GIFTED

A NOVEL

Stephen Debonrepos

Acknowledgments

I would like to thank Tina Rubin, Sara Safari,
LK and my beta readers for their invaluable counsel, but
most of all, my wonderful girlfriend
and ace editor, Nicole Brechka

Table of Contents

Prologue 7

Chapter 1- Kid, You're A Natural 11

Chapter 2 - Tough Crowd 23

Chapter 3 - Footrubs and Summoning Bells 31

Chapter 4 - I Want You for My Birthday 37

Chapter 5 - Enter Shredder 41

Chapter 6 - Beverly 51

Chapter 7 - Babysitting 57

Chapter 8 - I Don't Like Your Surprises 61

Chapter 9 - Intro to Print Illustration 67

Chapter 10 - Bridget's Party 73

Chapter 11- Treasures, Old and New 79

Chapter 12 - Little Brown Bottles 83

Chapter 13 - 'Round the Clock Dini Topp 91

Chapter 14 - Plagiarism 95

Chapter 15 - Sleeping in Cars 101

Chapter 16 - Where Were You Eight Months Ago? 109

Chapter 17 - Integrity is Everything 113

Chapter 18 - Fortress Around Your Heart 121

Chapter 19 - Think Degas 127

Chapter 20 - Dean's Party 133

Chapter 21 - The *Paint It Black Magazine* Illustration Workshop 139

Chapter 22- The *Paint It Black Magazine* Workshop, Day 2 ... 145

Chapter 23 - Walking the Freeways 151

Chapter 24 - Mix Tape 157

Chapter 25 - Nothing Fancy 159

Chapter 26 - Help Wanted 163

Chapter 27 - We're Not All Cut Out to Be Mothers 171

Chapter 28 - Camelot! 175

Chapter 29 - It's *Prowst*.. 183

Chapter 30 - Bobby... 187

Chapter 31 - Post-Modern Art History 191

Chapter 32 - Digger, We Can't Do This Anymore.................. 195

Chapter 33 - A Real Meal.. 199

Chapter 34 - Threads 203

Chapter 35 - Feel the Bone! Draw the Flesh, but Feel the Bone!
.... 211

Chapter 36 - Money, Real Money 219

Chapter 37 - Drawings, and Other Things in Need of Fixing . 223

Chapter 38 - A Deadly Decision.. 227

Chapter 39 - The Swindle.. 229

Chapter 40 - Tailing Dini Topp 237

Chapter 41 - Off the Beaten Path....................................... 239

Chapter 42 - Out the Door 245

Chapter 43 - Candles and Linens. Hobnobbin'! 249

Chapter 44 - Allergies.. 253

Chapter 45 - Cool Like That... 257

Chapter 46 – Blackout...I Am Really Going to Enjoy This.... 261

Chapter 47 - Waking Up is Hard to Do (or Bad Wake Up) 267

Chapter 48 - Breaking News! 271

Chapter 49 - Tying Up Loose Ends 277

Chapter 50 - Murmurs and Whispers.................................. 283

Chapter 51 - You Know Who Did It, Don't You? 287

Chapter 52 - Onward 291

About the Author 299

Prologue

Happy Birthday! You Are Now a Man!

"Happy birthday, dear Digger! Happy birthday to you!"

The server brought out a scoop of rainbow sherbet with a candle sticking out of it and placed it in front of Digger. A single mylar balloon, tied to his chair, hung in the air. It had Batman on it. It turned slowly in space, looking for more interesting events in the large dining room.

It was 1985, and Digger's family was celebrating his eighteenth birthday at Steak Corral restaurant. They applauded as they chanted, "Make a wish! Make a wish!"

"Wha'd you wish for?" asked his mother with a forced joviality.

Digger was in agony. The kabuki theater of this family "celebration" was grueling. Everybody read the same birthday script. He could practically mouth the words spoken along with the speaker. Digger was a lean—some might say skinny—young man for whom shaving had not yet become all that necessary. There was something hard, yet boyish, about his face, like a young Lindsey Buckingham.

He found the whole thing embarrassing, from the juvenile balloon to the budget "family" restaurant.

Digger's divorced father was late, as usual. When he finally arrived, he sauntered in and gave Digger a greeting card. Inside was $100 along with some joke about finally being *legal*.

Digger's sister Audrey read the card.

"Hey, Dad, since when are *you* the big spender?" Audrey made the comment without it rippling her stoic face. "Oh, that's right. Your shit-eating grin is there because you won't have to pay child support anymore."

"The months that you bothered to send it," added mother, before gulping down her Diet Coke.

"You know the deal, right, Digger? You either set out and get your own place, or you start paying rent, helping out. Isn't that right?" Dad said.

"Yes, Dad."

"You know what time it is? It's time for presents!" Mom announced.

Digger got a red skinny leather tie with paint splotches all over it, like a Jackson Pollock, from his mother, as well as a small used color TV that she got from a real estate client who was moving out of state.

Digger stared at the tie as if it were a two-day-old fish.

"See? It has paint all over it, 'cause you're an artist!" said mother.

"There is no way in hell he is wearing that," Audrey cackled.

"What? It's hip! It's stylish! Why wouldn't he wear it?" Mother turned to Digger. "You'd wear it, wouldn't you?"

"Hell, I'd wear it," contributed Dad, reaching for the beer the server had placed in front of him.

Audrey got Digger a cassette case that looked like a briefcase and held one hundred tapes. Inside the case were three brand new tapes: the Police *Synchronicity*, Dire Straits *Brothers in Arms,* and Talking Heads *Little Creatures*.

"This is great, Audrey. Thanks."

Mother was stiff in the presence of the man who had run off with a younger woman. She overdid the *I'm fine, I'm over it,* act. Her tight smile was the sort she gave when trying to spoon-feed a baby smashed peas.

Digger's sketchbook lay on the table. Dad snatched it up and flipped through it, making Digger feel violated, as if he'd barged in on Digger taking a bath.

"Hey, why don't you draw me?"

"You should draw all of us!" exclaimed Mother, clasping her hands together. Digger's hands turned into fists below the dining table.

"Yeah," chimed Audrey sarcastically, "a big happy family portrait."

"Make me look like Burt Reynolds. Or, or Tom Selleck!" chirped dad.

Digger'd had it. He finally snapped.

"I'm not a show pony, or an organ grinder's monkey! You don't just snap your fingers, and it's *Draw, Digger, Draw!* Besides the point, no one is ever happy with their own likeness!"

The table went silent.

"You should be ashamed of yourself," admonished Mother. "What you have is a God-given talent. You should feel happy that people want you to draw for them."

"And usually free of charge," observed Digger.

"It's his birthday! Shit, let him do what he wants!" piffed Audrey.

"What the fuck is wrong with you, Digger!" yelled Mother. "We were all having a good time, and you have to spoil it with your fucking attitude!"

"Eighteen! You're a man now, Digger," chimed in Father. "So, how does it feel to be a man?"

Chapter 1- Kid, You're A Natural

Digger had fallen in love twice in his life; once with music and once with drawing.

Since childhood, his head had never been quiet. Whether it was a song or an idea, his mind always crackled. It raced, and it spun. It was a pinball, banking and slamming from one subject to another at cracking speed. Thinking was all he did and he never clocked out. It was a slippery thing, his mind. It went wherever it wanted, as if he had little say in the matter.

"Crap. I'm gonna be late for class." Digger checked his wristwatch in the darkroom. It was ten minutes 'til quitting time, and he needed to wrap up shooting this graphic of a monster truck so that it could go on the silkscreens in time for the swing shift. The boss did not like paying one minute of unauthorized overtime.

Digger worked in a balloon factory in Walnut, CA, ten hours a day, six days a week. He'd initially been hired for the darkroom, but there was only so much darkroom work per day and plenty of warehouse work to be done. So, he spent most of his time on the factory floor, hauling and hoisting boxes, counting, weighing, and packing balloons.

This graphic had to be shot, developed, and burned onto four different silkscreens so that the women on the "floor" could print this or that company logo or birthday greeting on the custom balloons in time for FedEx.

"Yeah, I know. I know," Digger told Bill, the shipping clerk, as Bill barged into the darkroom. "I want to get out of here, too. I've got class tonight."

"Since when do you have class?" Bill joked. "Hurry up, so I can lock up the darkroom. I'm going to Vegas for the weekend. Taking tomorrow off. My wife and I have tickets for the Pointer Sisters!" Bill said this last bit as an obvious bid to impress.

Bill was Hawaiian, with a shaved, high, round skull and rimless glasses.

"You know, Bill, it would make more sense to just give me keys to the darkroom."

By the time Digger had completed his sentence, Bill was already gone.

*

Driving his VW Bus at magic hour, Digger again checked the time on his watch. Now, he was *really* running late. Riding high on a freeway arc, Digger felt as though he were piloting the bus through the glowing orange sky. He perused the cassette organizer he'd gotten for his birthday between the bus seats and popped a Dire Straits tape into the deck. *Walk of Life* began to whistle through the speakers. He banged his fist on the steering wheel in time with the music, beeping his horn here and there.

Man! This is a great song. Digger was living the life. He had a job and his own money, a bus that ran most of the time to get him wherever he wanted to go, and he was good at something, *really* good at something. Ever since high school, he was *That Artist Guy,* and he loved it. This freedom was new, which made it all the shinier.

He looked at his watch again. *Late late late.* He hated being late. Being late was not keeping your word. Mother had taught him this.

He pulled into the Sip N' Snak and grabbed a couple of microwave burritos with the money he kept in a coffee can, also between the car seats.

"Fill 'er up," he told the cashier, sliding a fistful of crumpled bills and coins toward them. "Pump six."

Digger opened the small metal door on the bus and inserted the fueling nozzle. He began to speak to the air as he slammed the lever on the gas pump, activating the numbers that tumbled like a slot machine. As he often did, he interviewed himself... just for practice.

"No, no, no. I don't *see* it before I put it on paper. I just know what to put down. I know it like I know my own phone number. I don't *see* my own phone number. I just know it. I put down a line, then I decide what should go next. It's all improvisation, really. It's like music... or math."

Back in the car, Digger resumed interviewing himself.

"You see, the word *genius* throws people. It's like saying *student.* When you think of a student, you could be thinking of an infinite variety of people, their majors being just the start of it all. Excuse me? That's a good question. I don't think of myself as a genius," Digger chuckled. "That's like knighting yourself. I'll leave that for others to decide," Digger concluded with requisite modesty.

In the cement hallway of the junior college, a large and ratty bulletin board snagged Digger's eye.

3x5 index cards listed rooms for rent, $600 cars, and ride shares to Berkeley. Flyers promoted local bands playing keggers. There was also a flyer offering a semester of study in Spain.

A pushpin held a fan of Design Center brochures. Digger's eyes flashed at the sight of them. He took one and flipped through it, as if he didn't want anyone to notice.

Design Center in Pasadena was the Mecca of commercial, industrial, and fine art study. It was a rich kids' school, but the artwork that came out of there was spectacular. If you went there, that meant that you were good. If you came out of there, that meant that you were great.

That's all Digger wanted, was to be Great, not just Design Center great, but look-him-up-in-the-footnotes great.

He didn't want to be a household name like Norman Rockwell (who himself was no slouch, despite being remembered for all of his kitschy Americana). He wanted to get the nod from his heroes that, yes, he was the *real deal*. He wanted to have bulletproof chops and the recognition that comes with Genius. He didn't dare admit this aloud, but it was true. He yearned for greatness, if only in the eyes of the few, those who mattered.

He feared being discovered, not as a joke —he knew he wasn't that—but as a *near miss*. That was his biggest fear.

He was yet a kid. Yes, he was good. He was very good. But, he wanted to be Great.

He slipped the brochure into his sketchbook.

A large and lush poster caught his eye. It was for the Design Center "*Paint It Black Magazine* Winter Illustration

Workshop." It was striking in its slashing grey and orange shapes.

Digger entered the large studio classroom with its high ceiling, carrying his Aero-Lite drawing board and a cigar box full of drawing materials bound by a rubber band. He gave a lift of the chin to a couple of his fellow students.

Some huddled around plastic-lined trash cans, using razor blades and X-Acto knives to shave the wood off their charcoal pencils. Some were deadly serious in their concentration, while others gossiped about the day's events.

Large student paintings leaned against the racks that housed even more legions of paintings, in varying degrees of dryness. Figure drawings were pinned to the walls.

The eyes of a sweatshirted young woman wandered as she sharpened her charcoal pencil.

"Hey! Watch it!" admonished another girl in braids. "An X-Acto is as sharp as a razor blade."

"But five times as strong," another student chimed in. "Lop your thumb right off."

Wearing only a silk dressing robe, a drooping female model in her early thirties emerged from behind a Japanese dressing screen and took the stand. Students not already straddling their wooden "horses," benches made specifically for figure drawing, did so now.

The model removed and laid her robe onto a chair. She was now nude. She was slender, but not a fashion-model type. A little doughy, she had the idiosyncratic dips and bulges of an ordinary person.

She assumed a wan pose with her left arm across her body and her left hand grasping her opposite shoulder.

"Is this okay?" she asked the room. The room mumbled varying levels of approval.

"Looks great!" said Judy, an older student with spiky blonde white hair and a flipped-up collar.

Digger was uneasy. He didn't like the pose. It was weak. He intervened.

"Could you...?" Digger stood and placed his own hands on his hips, canting his hips and shoulders in a more *contrapposto* pose, demonstrating what he wanted for the model. There. That was it.

"There he is, Mister Celebrity," Judy muttered under her breath. "Mister Know-It-All."

Walt, a lanky Gary Cooper in his mid-sixties, entered the room, and the noise dropped drastically.

"Alright. Let's warm up with some short ones." Walt chewed his unlit pipe.

"Three tens and a fifteen!" pleaded one student.

"Five fives and two tens!" countered another.

"Okay," settled Walt. "We'll start with five fives, a ten, then a fifteen-minute pose."

Some students groaned at having less time for each warm-up pose. A few, however, including Digger, smiled at having more quick ones. He drew quickly, and the shorter poses sharpened his skills more because there were more of them. Walt had taught him that it was better to make more drawings than to make a career out of just one. It gave you mileage.

Walt set the timer. Thus, the session began.

Some blew out their cheeks. Some pushed their mouths completely to one side, trying to figure out how to even begin their drawings.

Digger squinted, taking in the pose. He cranked his head clockwise, then counterclockwise. He then straightened his back and made long and confident scrapes on the large drawing pad that rested on his thighs.

Digger's wrist flicked left and right like a switchblade in a French 60s movie. He was good. Usually, most of the other students just steered clear of him. But, sometimes … they didn't.

Student Trish sat next to Digger. She leaned over toward him.

"Excuse me?" Trish asked Digger.

"I'm having trouble with the shoulder blade area," she whispered. "I just can't seem to get it right."

"Let's take a look," Digger answered in a hushed tone. He got up and sat at her horse, scanning the troubled drawing. He picked up her pencil and asked her, "Mind if I draw on your pad?" Digger tried not to ogle Trish out of the corner of his eye. She *was* fetching.

One of the things Walt taught Digger was studio etiquette. You never touched a model, especially when they were disrobed. If you needed to alter the pose, you did it by suggestion and demonstration. You asked permission before touching the drawing of another.

"No! Please do!" Trish was eager, maybe desperate.

Digger settled in then arched his back, pencil in hand.

"Boy. A lot going on here," Digger said, rubbing his chin.

Trish's drawing was a bubbling mess of colliding tumors riding along the shoulder blade.

Trish put her fists to her temples. She was overwhelmed, lost.

"Looks like you've been studying some anatomy," observed Digger, surveying Trish's handiwork. "A little learning is a dangerous thing," Digger quoted. "Okay. Forget the anatomy for now. Let's draw what we see."

Trish nodded. A few students gathered behind the two of them.

"All your muscles along the shoulder blade here are shouting at once. What you see and what you know should take turns; they should inform each other, but they can't talk at the same time. That bulge you *see* there—"

Digger now spoke more loudly, clearly, in order to benefit the crowd that had amassed around him. He waved the charcoal pencil just above the pad, indicating the troubled area.

"—informs you to emphasize the muscle that you *know*, a muscle that attaches … here," Digger marked the paper. "and here." He marked it again.

"It doesn't matter if it's a pencil mark or a piece of chewing gum, so long as the eye stops… here. It has to *feel* that bone."

Trish nodded along with several others.

"You don't want clutter. You want savoir faire. You want to show some," Digger double raised his eyebrows at her, "taste." Trish smiled warmly.

Digger knew that he had a useful amount of charm that served him from time to time.

He brought the pencil to hover over the large pad, over an empty patch of the page in the lower corner.

He then laid in some elegant wisps, then banged in a few accents.

Some viewed with wonder, some with contempt. This was Saturday Night Fever, and Digger had taken the floor. He was young and in his element, king of the roost, strutting his stuff. He was a hotshot, and he just loved it.

"Oh, God," moaned Trish. "I don't know anything."

"You know a lot. You just don't need to give it all to us at once. Save something for the honeymoon."

Digger and Trish exchanged smiles. He was putting her at ease.

"You don't have to try so hard. Speak less. Say more."

"Less is more," echoed Trish. Digger shrugged.

"Close enough."

Digger dismounted the horse and began to leave as the small audience tightened around the freshly completed demo drawing.

Contemptuous Judy chimed in.

"And just what are your credentials to teach?" Judy asked.

Walt heard this and took an interest. An electronic timer went off, signaling the end of the last pose.

"Coffee break, everybody," Walt announced. "Don't forget to come back."

Digger pointed to his own drawing on his horse, which had admirers clustered around it. He addressed Judy without looking at her.

"There. Those are my credentials."

Students milled around the classroom, silently scrutinizing the drawings that had not been flipped over so as not to be seen, while the others praised, encouraged, and consoled each other.

Walt and Digger drifted to the open back door, where Walt could smoke his pipe. A family of raccoons descended the hills and took a right.

"Kid. You're a natural," said Walt. "Here. Take this."

Walt handed Digger a brochure of the Design Center at Night program, just like the ones on the bulletin board, just like the one that Digger already took.

"Design Center. They're more hardcore there. Better models, too."

"I like it here," said Digger, telling a half-truth.

"You've outgrown this place. There's nothing here for you anymore. You're sharp, but a head start's only good for so long," warned Walt.

"Looks expensive."

"Check it out, kid."

"If you say so, Walt."

"Don't play it cool, kid. You must be dyin' to go to a place like this."

"I don't have any money, Walt." Digger's voice wavered, surprising him.

"Where there's a will, there's a way, kid. Check it out."

"I will, Walt."

*

Back in the parking lot. Digger's bus wouldn't start. *Oh, just great.*

Digger sat for a bit, cross-legged on the ground, picking at the strands of grass that broke through the asphalt, wondering what to do.

Calling his mother or his sister, Audrey, wasn't an option. They had often proven that they just couldn't care less. Digger watched his breath curl in the air.

He hoofed it to a payphone next to the guard station and called Kevin's house. Levi, the night security guard for the north parking lot, came out to make sure that Digger was okay, then returned to his post.

Luckily, Kevin's mom said he was at the campus computer lab.

Digger hiked across campus, hoping to find him.

*

Kevin fished some jumper cables out of the trunk of his big old boat of a car, while Digger popped the hood.

Digger's best friend, Kevin, wore an army surplus field jacket covered in patches and a mop of curly black hair. The patches ranged from flower symbols to peace symbols.

After putting the clamps on the battery terminals, Kevin got into his car and started it up.

He revved the engine for a bit.

"Okay, Digger! Go!"

Digger tried his car. It started right up.

Kevin left his car running as he came to Digger's window.

"I'm hungry. What do you say, Digger, Carrows?"

"My treat."

Digger thought of Judy, the obnoxious woman from class.

He also thought of X-Acto blades. They were as sharp as scalpels.

21

Chapter 2 - Tough Crowd

Carrows was open 24 hours, the perfect place for late-night cram and study sessions. It was after midnight on a weeknight, so it was fairly quiet. Only a few tables were occupied.

Digger and Kevin took up a booth piled high with books. Kevin poked the innards of a dissected electronic gadget.

"Kevin, didn't you just get that for Christmas?"

"Don't worry. I'll get it back together."

"What is *this*?" Digger picked up a big, blue hardback book from Kevin's stack.

"It's a copy of the DSM-III. I picked it up at the used bookstore across the street from the college. It's the Diagnostic and Statistical Manual of Mental Disorders."

"Any good?" asked Digger, flipping through it.

"Pretty good. I'm reading about PTSD. It's when someone relives trauma or keeps it with them ongoing, like if you went to war or grew up in a really abusive home."

"Hmmm…"

"That's *you*, friend."

"*Me?* I don't think so."

"Well, *I* think so."

"Yes, my mom can be obnoxious, but—"

A sturdy, professionally chipper waitress in her early thirties showed up to take their orders.

"Okay, gents. What can I do you for?"

"We'll have the fried zucchini and nachos," began Digger, perusing the menu unnecessarily. They were there most nights and knew the menu by heart.

"And an iced tea, no lemon, please," ordered Digger.

"A Please and Thank You Man. Love that," answered the waitress. Her name tag read "Karen."

"And I'll have a Coke and a chocolate shake with floor wax," deadpanned Kevin.

"And one," said the waitress, jotting, "floor wax. Got it."

"Thank you, Ma'am," concluded Digger.

"Ma'am, even. I think I'm in love. Call me Karen. Okay, I'll be right back with your drinks."

Digger stared at the *Paint It Black Magazine* Workshop brochure.

"What's that, Dee-gur?" Kevin pronounced his friend's name like Col. Klink on Hogan's Heroes.

"It's a brochure for an illustration workshop. Man, this looks cool."

Just then, four brash street toughs—three male, one female— burst through the front door. Their movements were loud and jarring. They weren't just loud, they were dangerous, the kind of young, hormone-fueled sociopaths who targeted vulnerable people like Digger and Kevin, who stiffened at the sight of them.

They wore leather and denim. Had piercings and tattoos.

One sat high on the back of the booth's bench seat. He was rugged-looking with a short mullet. The girl had a shock of bleached white hair and thick eyeliner. She wore a black Lynyrd Skynyrd T-shirt with the sleeves torn off. Another was skinny and wore sunglasses indoors. The last guy was a tank. He had worn a denim vest and a beard.

"And of course, they're wearing hats indoors," began Kevin. "I wish I had a flame thrower."

The unruly table of toughs erupted into laughter over something. They used loud profanity. A patron from another table turned her head, then back, clearly disapproving.

"*I* wish you had a flame thrower."

"Assholes," responded Kevin.

"The world has no use for people like them. I'd like to take a razor blade and slice them thinly like a big clove of garlic."

Digger looked up from his pad. He inadvertently made eye contact with one of the tough guys, the leader, who gave him a direct and territorial stare.

Tough One unexpectedly put his hands together in a praying position. He yelled out to Digger.

"Oh! So sorry! Did we interrupt your meal? Were we being too *loud*?" With that, they burst into laughter. It died quickly. "You want to do something about it, Poindexter?"

Tough Guy slapped his table, causing Digger to jump.

The manager poked his head into the dining area, perhaps deciding whether or not to call the cops.

The toughs retreated their focus back to their own table.

Karen, the waitress, brought the Coke and iced tea. Digger extracted the lemon from his iced tea and put it to the side.

"They never get it right here," complained Kevin, "If you say, no cheese, it comes with cheese. You say extra pickles, it doesn't happen."

"Damn it. I need a haircut," complained Digger, trying to ignore and simultaneously monitor the creepy gang of toughs. "It keeps touching my ears. I hate that."

As the toughs noisily vacated their booth, Karen began to bus their table. They had left a pile of crumpled bills and a handful of change on the plastic tip tray. Karen stared into nearby space as if trying to guess the weight of the tray she held in her hands.

Karen swung by Digger and Kevin.

"What's fifteen percent of twenty-four- four, seventy-one?"

Digger and Kevin answer in unison.

"Three dollars, seventy cents and two-thirds."

"What is a buck, eighty-two of twenty-four, seventy-one?

"A shitty tip," answered Kevin.

"You some kind of math geniuses?"

"I'm a polymath," said Kevin.

"Which means—"

"Which means," explained Kevin, "I'm kick-ass at pretty much whatever I do."

"Huh. And how 'bout you?" Karen asked Digger.

"I'm his entourage."

Karen nodded, then set off to refill coffees at other tables.

Digger picked up Kevin's library copy of a book on medieval torture while Kevin milled over a Daredevil comic book. Digger copied the illustrations from the torture book.

"Frank Miller was twenty-four when he got his big break drawing *Daredevil*, Digger. You better get a move on, buddy."

Digger's skin tightened.

"Clock's a tickin'," Kevin continued. "You've only got so long to make your mark before you're just another nut job shaking his fist at the TV."

Digger's sketchbook lay open, along with copies of *Drawing the Head and Hands* by Andrew Loomis, *Bridgman's Constructive Anatomy,* and *How to Draw Comics the Marvel Way*, his personal bible.

The sketchbook's flayed bodies recalled the Spanish Inquisition. These were violent and disturbing images, complicated structures of wood and iron, designed to pull confessions from the fallen, rendered in knowing detail.

"Whoa. Scary stuff," observed Karen. "So, you're a draw-er. My cousin used to be a draw-er."

"Draughtsman," corrected Digger.

"What?"

"Draughtsman. Someone who draws at a high level of skill is a draughtsman. A 'draw-er' is where you keep your panties."

"I keep my panties in my purse," Karen teased and refilled Digger's iced tea.

"So, an artist," she continued. "Always wanted to be an artist. I can't draw a straight line with a ruler."

"I use a ruler," said Digger. "Anyway, I'm not an artist. I'm just a student."

"You just sit in a classroom, drawing naked ladies all day?"

"And men." Kevin offered.

"And men?"

*

In the back of the Carrows parking lot, Digger, Kevin, and Karen the Waitress, taking her break, stood beside the back of Digger's VW Bus. Digger popped the back open and dragged out his thick drawing board and pad.

Karen, making ooh-ahh noises, selected from a thick stack of nude male charcoal drawings.

"Okay. I'll take these two. Oh. And this one. Gotta have this one. Lordy. Gotta have. Lord, have mercy."

"Hold on, now. That one … That's a good one. That's gonna cost you." Kevin intervened.

"Oh. Don't you two worry. I'll treat you right. For the next two weeks, I'll be feeding you better than your mommas."

Karen the Waitress carefully carried her new prized possessions to her car, shaking her head.

Digger turned to Kevin.

"Walt thinks I should check out Design Center."

"You should, Digger. I've heard about that place," Kevin said. "You don't realize how really good you are."

"I know how good I are."

"As good as you think you are, trust me, Digger, you're better."

The four boisterous toughs from inside earlier hung out around a bulky pick-up truck, standing high off the ground, decorated with AC/DC and Jack Daniels stickers.

One of them pointed to Digger.

"That's the one. The one with a staring problem."

Pumped and amused, Tough Guy One strutted before his pals, toward Digger and Kevin.

"Oh yeah, little faggot? You like to stare? You want to stare at me? You want to stare at her? You want to fuck my girl, you little faggot?"

Then, as if a sheet were pulled off a painting, Tough Guy's face revealed a charmer's smile.

"Hey, man! Just kidding! Just a little foolin' around. No hard feelings, eh?"

Suddenly, Tough Guy popped Digger in the nose. It burst like a bottle of ketchup.

Kevin was powerless. He just stood there, enraged by his own helplessness.

Digger then received a kick to the gut. Tough Guy's friends cheered.

He was slumped on the ground with his back toward Kevin and the toughs. When he turned around without getting up, Digger saw Tough Guy pick up his sketchbook off the asphalt.

"Lookie, lookie here." Tough Guy One began to flip through the sketch diary unceremoniously. He squinted at one of the pages and slowly read, "'Lastissimus Dorsi.'"He then burst into laughter. "What the fuck? What the fuck is a Lastissimus Dorsi?" He turned to his buddies who egged him on, whooping and hollering.

Digger muttered something.

"What was that? You say something?" Tough Guy made a show of tearing out a page.

"It's a muscle, you ape."

"Oh, it's a *muscle*. Hear that, guys? It's a muscle!" He tore out another page.

Neither Digger nor Kevin dared move.

Tough Guy dropped the sketchbook to the ground then, unzipped his fly and urinated all over it.

"Whoops!" said Tough Guy as he zipped up. He backed a few steps, then with a cackle, turned around and rejoined his friends.

The Toughs laughed as they piled into the truck and drove away with their stereo blaring Led Zeppelin's *Whole Lotta Love*.

"You okay?" asked Kevin.

"My mom hits me harder." Digger joked, holding his nose.

Digger was enraged. He was humiliated. He wanted to cry. He wanted to kill.

"That would be funny if I didn't know your mother," said Kevin. "I hate this town.

Chapter 3 - Footrubs and Summoning Bells

Digger snuck into his dark house through the back door. His nose had stopped bleeding, but there was still some blood on his shirt.

On the wall hung some family photos, the usual display. There was also a pastel portrait. It was of his mother. She was made to look ten years younger and ten pounds lighter. Mother was vain, and Digger knew better than not to flatter her.

The ringing of a small brass handbell stopped Digger in his tracks. *Oh, Christ*, he thought.

The door cracked open, allowing a slim shaft of light into his mother's pitch black bedroom. Only the digital alarm clock glowed in the darkness.

"Yes, Mom?" queried Digger.

"Come, Digger. Rub my feet, will you?"

Mother lay in a huge bed with an elaborate mirrored headboard crammed with creams and lotions. She replaced the handbell on the headboard.

"I just got home," Digger moaned.

"Two seconds. It'll take *two seconds*. Quit your whining."

"Mom. It's 3 am. I'm tired. I have work tomorrow, and I need a haircut."

"You don't need a Goddamn haircut. I swear, you're not happy unless you're making yourself miserable."

Digger squirmed. "It's touching my ears."

Mother tossed a bottle of lotion to Digger. It hit him in the chin.

"Make sure to warm it up in your hands first," mother hissed. "Don't you put that freezing crap on my feet."

Digger kneaded his mother's feet, eliciting grotesque groans from her. These groans made him feel uneasy. These sounds should not be coming from one's mother.

"I'm an adult now. Please don't talk to me like that."

"Book-smart and people-stupid is what you are. Just like your father."

Digger looked to the ceiling, as if an answer lay there.

"This stuff smells like almonds, mother. You're allergic to nuts."

"For Christ sakes, Digger. I'm not going to eat it."

Digger knew this next part wouldn't be easy.

"Mom, my car wouldn't start. I think it's the alternator."

"Well, I'm not loaning you any money. You are an adult now, after all. Now, finish rubbing my feet. I have work too, you know."

"Yeah. Mother, there's another thing." Digger took a breath. "I want to go to the Design Center."

"The rich kids' school? Good luck with that."

"You know I don't have that kind of money."

"And you think I do? Look around you. We don't exactly live at the Playboy Mansion."

"I could get loans."

"And I suppose you would want me to co-sign for them. Go ask your father and let me get some rest, will you?" She was sounding exasperated.

Digger resumed his kneading, which got softer and softer as mother drifted off to sleep.

Mother was snoring now.

Digger, gauging that he'd logged enough time to slink away without penalty, cautiously pulled the bed comforter over Mother's feet, then made his way to the door, leaving the bedroom.

Before he made it out of the door, he heard his mother's voice.

"I told Monica you'd babysit for her Friday night." Monica was one of my mother's best friends.

"You did what? Without even asking me?"

"Oh, don't get all bent out of shape. It's not on a school night, and besides, you'll make a few bucks."

"A few is right."

"There you go with that smart mouth."

"Goddamn it, you can't *do* that! You gotta *ask* me first."

"I told Monica you'd be there at 7:30."

Digger was furious. His head was hot, and there was nothing he felt he could do to stop her. His breathing grew ragged, and his eyes grew wet. He wanted his mother dead.

He was powerless. She was always doing stuff like this. She had absolutely no respect for Digger, had zero boundaries, and all Digger could do was cower. Why, oh why, couldn't he just tell her to fuck off?

Digger left her room and went across the house and down the hall to his. He was abuzz now. There was no way he could go to sleep.

He sat down at his makeshift art table and tried to get just a little bit of drawing in before falling into bed like a log.

He was adding the final highlights to a monochromatic pastel portrait. It was of a shampoo ad from a magazine, but using the lighting from a book on Caravaggio. His small TV was on low. Since his room was at the far end of the house, he could usually run it without anybody hearing.

Mother entered without knocking, startling Digger, causing him to jump.

"You can't talk that way to me, Digger. I won't tolerate the disrespect."

She took an interest in Digger's drawing.

"What is this?' she asked, looking slightly lecherous. "This for school?"

"No, just practice," said Digger, sounding slightly embarrassed.

"Why is it all purple? Well, it's gonna look great on the living room wall. Go ahead and sign it."

"That's not going on any wall. It's mine, and besides, it's not very good. By the way, signing your work is tacky nowadays."

"Not very good? It looks exactly like a Renaissance drawing! Look. You're *my* son, and I'm going to have that on my wall."

With that, Mother pushed past Digger, untaped the drawing from its board, and took possession of it.

She left the room, and Digger sat there, fazed. He took out the Design Center brochure and looked it over longingly.

There was no way he was gonna make it to Design Center. They were notoriously tight with scholarships, and Digger's grades, despite whatever gifts he may have possessed, were nothing of note. He was trapped, and he was gonna stay trapped until he did something, something bold.

Chapter 4 - I Want You for My Birthday

The sign on the cosmetology school window read "$10 HAIRCUTS" and "FREE BLOW DRY."

Digger sat in a pneumatic chair while a big blonde woman pumped it with her foot, raising him to an acceptable height. With a flourish, she threw a plastic poncho onto Digger, fastening it tightly around the neck.

"I'm Bridget. I'll be your stewardess today," she introduced herself.

The smell of solvents and dyes stuffed the air. The whole place stabbed Digger's brain through the nose.

The bosomy woman examined Digger's unruly shock of hair.

"Real short. Over the ears," briefed Digger. "Think FBI, or Charles Lindbergh."

"Charles Lindbergh? There's a name I don't hear every day."

Digger snatched a ball-point pen and a junk mail envelope from Bridget's beauty station.

"If I may?" asked Digger.

Digger briskly began to sketch out a handsome 50s-style Madison Ave. man with a sharp haircut on the back of the envelope. "Like this."

"Ah, the artsy type. I like it," Bridget grinned.

He completed the sketch and showed it to her.

"Got it?"

"I gotcha."

The mirror's edge on Bridget's station was full of photos of friends, postcards, and mini-flyers. They suggested a heavy involvement in Community Theatre. Polaroids of her lacing up somebody's costume, some of her in group photos like in grade school, cast parties, shots of stage productions…

One in particular caught Digger's eye. It was a duo of postcards from Spain.

"Spain, huh?"

"You got it, cowboy. I *love* me some Spain. Wish I were back there right now."

He thought of mentioning his school's study abroad program, but thought better of it. He didn't want to come off as a kid. *Gee whiz! Our class is going to Spain, Bridget! Why don't you pat me on the head?!*

As Bridget spritzed his hair with a spray bottle, Digger picked up a women's magazine and read the title of the quiz aloud.

"*Ten Things All Men Should Know.* So, how true is this?"

"Any man who cares enough to ask, believe me, already knows plenty."

She cut a guideline in his hair, and Digger paid close attention. By watching, he was learning, always learning. Digger's attention to detail and to his surroundings was remarkable, if not amazing.

Digger flipped through the magazine.

"How old are you?" she asked.

"How old do I look? Digger flipped to an article on *Your Summer Body*.

"You *look* fifteen. Jesus. You're just a baby."

"Why, shucks, no. I've been on solid food for years, now."

"Off the nipple, eh?" Bridget was sold. This little charmer was something else.

"You know, you have a great forehead," complimented Digger.

"Do I?" responded Bridget.

"Here." Bridget scribbled her phone number on the envelope. She ripped it in half, giving the half with her number to Digger and stuffing the half with his haircut sketch into the breast pocket of her white smock.

"My birthday's this Saturday, and my folks'll be out of town. I'm having a 24th birthday party."

"And you'd like me as a guest? Why, I'm flattered."

"Guest, hell. Young man, you're my present."

Chapter 5 - Enter Shredder

Design Center was a massive, slick, and sterile, steel and glass structure that was once thought of as bold. But now its architectural ideas had been replicated so often that it seemed old hat. Through its slick and clean halls flowed snotty and pretentious brats, most of whom were there on daddy's dime.

A line of applicants trailed out of the registration office. A sign taped to the wall read "NIGHT PROGRAM REGISTRATION HERE." There were people aged eighteen to sixty-five. The night program culled folks from various stages of life and from various backgrounds. There were paint-splattered jeans, mini-skirts, slacks, and even a kilt. There were crew cuts, mohawks, ponytails, and those who defied any category of style.

"Next!" yelled the registrar.

Upon hearing this, Digger stepped to the counter and produced his paperwork.

"And how are you today?" Digger asked, as if their roles were reversed.

The registrar just grunted.

"There seems to be a mistake here." Digger pointed to a computer-printed form at the top of his stack.

"That's not my name," said Digger.

"Sure, it is. Says right there."

"No. But, it's not. I assure you, it's not."

Shaking her head, the registrar punched the keys on her computer, then heaved herself off her stool.

"Wait right here."

The registrar went to the noisy dot matrix printer to retrieve the corrected document.

"Easy mistake. Happens all the time. Happened at my last school," Digger explained, trying to lighten the mood. "And the last one."

The registrar returned.

"Okay. Here you go," said the registrar, handing Digger a paper class schedule.

"Intro to Print Illustration. Tuesday-Thursday. 7 to 10 p.m."

"Intro to Print Illustration? Isn't there a pure drawing class I could take?"

The registrar consulted her screen.

"Looks like they waived all of the prerequisites. Apparently, you can already draw. Intro to Print Illustration is the only studio night class you're eligible for. Don't worry. It's a good one. The credits'll transfer right over when you decide to apply as a full-time student."

Digger was visibly disappointed, if not outright angered. His features buckled into a tense frown. He didn't care about making images for magazine pieces on the economy. He just wanted to draw, to learn *about* drawing. There was a *lot* to learn.

Most people stopped learning when they could bang out an acceptable likeness or figure, but drawing was so much more. Walt had taught Digger that. He had given Digger a glimpse of a new universe, one of linear mechanics and tonal atmospheres. One of the muscle bulges and tendon insertions. It would be a lifelong path, not just a few tricks and gimmicks in order to impress your friends and neighbors.

Classical drawing was a language. Perhaps a dying language, but a language nevertheless. Perhaps it had dwindling practical relevance in the modern world, but it held tremendous personal value to its disciples, much like those who study a martial art deeply, beyond the mere idea of practical self-defense. It has lessons, lessons perhaps only truly appreciated by those of kindred spirits.

"There is, however," the registrar continued, "an afternoon figure workshop. It's free to students. It's uninstructed, but some of the teachers hang out there from time to time. It's already started today, but you still have time to check it out."

"Free? Even to night students?"

"I won't tell if you don't." She looked past Digger. "Next!"

*

After hurriedly grabbing his drawing gear from his VW bus, Digger frantically roamed the Design Center halls, looking for the drawing workshop. He walked briskly, as he knew he had missed at least some of it. He poked his head into each door.

Standing people lined the halls, advertising and promoting campus clubs and student credit cards, giving away Frisbees and T-shirts bearing corporate logos.

The gauntlet of barkers really hawked. It was frightening. One shoved a sheaf of credit card application brochures into Digger's hand. Not wanting to litter, he stuffed them into his shoulder bag.

Student credit cards. Yeah right. There was no way in hell he was going to fall for that. They charged loan shark interest rates, plus annual fees. Thanks, but no thanks. He was going to throw those applications into the trash the first chance he got.

Finally, there it was, Room 109. Digger stood just outside for a moment. He took a deep breath, then entered.

Feeling like a stowaway, Digger hoped no one would point him out as not belonging there.

There were the standard easels and horses, but this place was much tidier than the JC. From the looks of it, the caliber of drawing was a noticeable jump higher than that at the junior college.

People can get pretty territorial in a drawing class, and Digger wished he could have gotten there earlier. With a look, a cough, or a grunt, two different students told Digger, *Fuck off. You're too close. This is* my *space.*

They wore expensive new Walkman players and jotted notes into thick day-runners. They were quick, slick, and put-together. Digger felt outclassed and embarrassingly out of place.

Tony, an adorable guy with little round eyeglasses and a little round cap, greeted Digger. He wore a Design Center T-shirt.

"Hey, man. I don't know you. I'm Tony," offering his hand.

"Digger," accepting it.

Then there was Rachel, who looked like she colored her hair with maroon spray paint, and Jonny, who wore combat boots, a flight jacket with patches on the sleeves, and only peach fuzz on his head. They all seemed to know each other. They must have been full-timers.

"Digger? Whoa! That's a fucked up name. I mean, good fucked up. I mean. Never mind. Oh, shit. Here he comes!"

Digger turned to see what Tony was talking about.

"Here comes Pashone, The Shredder."

"Shredder?" Digger repeated.

Tony couldn't help but laugh as he spoke.

"Pashone teaches painting and drawing composition. He says the most fucked up shit. I swear. Jonny, what'd he say to you last time?"

"Oh yeah," Jonny said, "Shredder told me, You've got a lot of good ideas. ' "Jonny took a dramatic pause. "And you're not using any of them."

"Ooh! Shuh-redded!! Man! He is the shit! He's a fucking legend. Have you ever seen him draw? Holy shit!"

"First time I saw him draw, I wanted to suck his dick, right then and there," confessed Rachel.

"Shit! *I* wanted to suck his dick!" exclaimed Tony.

Digger gave Tony a glance, asking, *Are you?* to which Tony quickly shook his head, "No."

"Most of these guys here just write Shredder off," began Rachel. "They're just photography majors or here to get graphic design jobs at Target corporate or Hallmark or some shit. He doesn't make any sense to them. They just want to learn how to bang out some stick figures and move on."

"But, to us pencil geeks, drawing is a religion," said Tony. Digger nodded in ready approval. He liked what he was hearing. These were his kind of people.

Dean, with Norse good looks, hair slicked back into a blonde ponytail, and broad shoulders, entered.

"Uh oh! There's Dean!" exclaimed Tony.

"Oh, that dude." Jonny was clearly not a fan.

"Oh. Come on," defended Tony. "He's alright."

Dean made a show of choosing his spot. He used his hands like a film director to frame his shot on the model stand. Then, after dragging them across the cement floor, he stacked one horse upon another to sit way up high. Every move he made resulted in a tremendous amount of noise.

Digger's hands felt dirty. He headed over to the sink to wash them. He waited his turn behind a seemingly aimless housewife-type. She spoke to him over her shoulder.

"Come on. There's room. Hi. I'm Beverly." She extended a soapy hand.

Beverly had deeply intelligent eyes and the hard-won calm of a cancer survivor. She was older than most of the students, maybe mid-thirties, and she was tiny. Her shortish hair was both efficient and stylish.

A nude male model in his early forties, with the physique of a trained dancer, took the small stage and twisted himself into a gorgeous pose of torque and power, then held it perfectly still, save for his calm and controlled breathing. Now this was more like it! Not like those rag doll models at the junior college.

Henry Pashone took his place by his easel. He tucked one of his errant grey locks behind his ear and tilted his head slightly back to look through the lowered specs resting on his nose. He wore a fisherman's khaki vest that seemed entirely made of pockets.

"Fuck. I gotta see this," said Tony eagerly.

Tony hopped off his wooden horse, abandoning his own drawing, then stage tiptoed behind Pashone.

Even in his sixties, Pashone was Cary Grant dashing. His confident and efficient slashes against the drawing pad might as well be those of a Musketeer fencing. They elicited oohs and ahhhs from Tony.

Jonny couldn't help himself. He abandoned his own drawing pad and joined Tony in watching Pashone draw. Curious, Digger got up and joined them.

Waves of Pashone's hand left only the faintest traces of soft, seven-shaped lines on the rich Canson paper.

He hesitated, then dug and twisted his pencil in, carving and scooping until joints, elbows, and shoulders appeared on the page. Pashone pulled, in long strokes, the bulge and hang of muscles from the joint. He squinted at the model. He then switched to a white pencil and pulled a highlight out of the round mass of the shoulder.

Back to the charcoal, Pashone blocked in a mass of hair, barely indicating the curls of the model's locks. Pashone reassessed. He spoke out loud but softly, to those just around him as much as to himself.

"The figure looks complete, but the composition isn't *quite there* yet."

Pashone banged in a soft diagonal line and filled the shape with tone, separating light from shadow on the wall behind the model. Now, a quick suggestion of the stool beneath the model's bottom.

The drawing looked done to a breathless Tony and Jonny.

"Stop! Don't do any more!" begged Tony to himself.

"Don't mess it up. It's perfect," whispered Jonny.

Pashone went back into the drawing and swoop-swoop! Took the study to a new and higher level.

Tony and Jonny were collapsing into each other like stoners. Pashone had stopped. The drawing was now complete.

Pashone rested his charcoal pencil on the lip of the easel and ambled away. Tony and Jonny let out a breath like they'd been holding it the whole time.

"Okay," commanded Pashone. "Let's break for ten."

Most of the students headed for the cafeteria, although many hung around the classroom, meandering around, checking out each other's drawings.

"I'm frickin' starving," said Tony, sliding his tray along. "I've got classes from 9 am, all the way until 10 at night."

"Did you see that drawing Shredder made? Holy fuck!" Jonny laughed at the sheer awesomeness of it. Rachel plucked a cranberry muffin from the selection.

"A muffin! Now we're talking!" Tony grabbed himself a blueberry muffin and began to tear off the top.
"Oh, man. Shredder is king. Did you see that thigh? You could feel the weight of it, the sheer *bulk* of it, without it being... I dunno... *bulky*."

"He is amazing."

The four of them took their coffee and snacks to the table closest to the door, right under a clock.

"So Diggs, when you gonna go full-time so we can hang out?" asked Jonny, leaning back in his chair.

"Yeah, Digger," chimed Tony.

"Still working out the details."

"You should come," Tony continued. "It'll totally kick your ass, but it's awesome."

"Sleep now, while you can," Rachel half-joked.

"You got *that* right," Tony and Jonny agreed.

"Maybe I could work while I came here."

"What, are you kidding? Tons of people don't even *make* it through here without the distractions of a job."

Just then, Digger realized just how much he had put his foot in his mouth, how he must have sounded to these rich kids who probably never had to work a job they didn't *want*.

"Shit. We'd better get back." The clock had taken mercy on poor Digger.

After the break, Pashone sat out the next pose. He made the rounds, hands behind his back, casually, and seemingly disinterestedly, monitoring the progress of the room.

He waved a finger over the drawing that belonged to a girl who wore a ponytail and a Walkman. She buried her eyes in her fists.

Pashone neared Tony, who now slaved away at a fresh figure study, and softly said something to him, without gesticulation.

As soon as the instructor turned his back, Tony doubled over in stage laughter. Digger looked to Tony for clarification. Tony mouthed, *Tell you later*.

Pashone got to Digger's drawing and stopped. He settled into a more comfortable stance and continued to stare, now with a loose fist raised to his mouth.

Other people in the room started to notice. This was not usual. Digger had no idea what he was awaiting.

"Well," said Pashone, quietly as he walked away. "You can certainly draw."

Those within earshot were left with their jaws hanging open.

Dean picked up on this.

"No way," Tony mouthed with a smile.

Tony then happily got back to work, touching up his own drawing.

Beverly stopped all of a sudden, like a cat who has just remembered something. Hers was the face of burden. She gathered her things quietly and efficiently and left the room.

Digger saw this. Why couldn't she stand to be in the room any longer?

Chapter 6 - Beverly

Beverly's pumps made a clip-clop sound against the cement floors of the Design Center hallway. On her right was a wall of lockers, absolutely unmolested by graffiti, painted a soothing mid-tone neutral grey. She appreciated the calm of her surroundings. She needed soothing, something to even out her breathing.

She walked dazed, as if set in motion years ago. She was recognized by the mildly dowdy Helen.

"Beverly! Beverly! Hey! Oh, hey." Helen's tone softened. "I just wanted to say, I just feel so awful for you. I'm so, so sorry for your …loss."

Beverly nodded as if enduring Thanksgiving with the in-laws.

"My god, Beverly. It must be so hard. I mean, I can only imagine—

Beverly looked slightly relieved. *Maybe. Just maybe. Maybe somebody, even slightly, understands.*

"How hard it must be," Helen continued.

Finally, somebody understands.

"to lose a child."

"Child," Beverly responded. "Oh yes. A child." She fished her sunglasses out of her purse. "Look, Helen. I really have to be somewhere. I'll call you."

"Certainly. Certainly, Beverly."

In the parking lot, getting into her Volvo, Beverly saw a slick beneath her car—an oil leak. *Oh great. One more fucking thing.*

With much more force than necessary, Beverly slammed her car door shut.

Why now? Why ever?

*

Beverly entered her hillside home and placed her keys in the decorative ceramic dish on the small cherry wood table that stood next to the front door, solemnly. Efficient Beverly removed her jacket and put it on the coat rack. *Good girl,* she told herself.

She had left her drawing items in the car and now had empty hands.

What to do with these empty hands?

She looked at her wrists, so pale, so fragile. But, no, not yet.

She looked over at the television. A frivolous distraction. Maybe even fun. No. Not fun. She didn't deserve fun. She didn't deserve wine either, but by George, that was on the bill tonight.

She pulled a bottle of red and poured herself a respectable measure.

Beverly looked out the back door onto the patio for one of the neighborhood cats who would sometimes come in for food, then curl up in her lap. No dice.

She took her wine to the recliner. The sofa was much too large for one person. You needed another person. You needed Peter.

Peter. Handsome Peter. Charming Peter. Sexy Peter. Smart as fucking shit, Peter.

Peter's picture stood by the phone on the end table. Beverly picked it up and held it.

Peter wasn't a matineé idol. He had the boy-next-door good looks that come with tousled hair and dimples.

She placed the picture back, faced down.

Just for a moment, she had the idea of running up the stairs and putting on one of his shirts, but no. Not now. She didn't deserve his smell.

Beverly had met Peter at a bookstore book sale. They had reached for the same book, the last copy of *The Collected Works of Rilke*, and he offered to let her take it.

They soon began a playful volley of Leonard Cohen quotes.

When he said he had to go—he had a class to TA— Beverly stopped him and asked him to dinner. She surprised herself. Not even his phone number, she had thought to herself, but an invitation to dinner. *Pretty bold, Beverly. Pretty, pretty bold.*

A few days later, one of them suggested pizza, and the other one vetoed it.

They wound up ordering Indian takeout and bringing it back to her apartment, where they spent the evening reading aloud to each other. Poems, passages from favorite books…

Beverly fell head over heels for him. His arms were the first place she ever felt so warm, so safe.

She never pushed for marriage. *Don't fuck with the magic*, she told herself. But when he produced a ring over a restaurant dinner on her October birthday, she said yes before he could finish asking.

They married on Valentine's Day in a small ceremony that was all Beverly needed.

Peter was not frivolous. It was easy for the two of them to scrape up a down payment for a cozy house on the hill. *I could be happy for the rest of my life like this. Don't change a thing,* she told herself. *Don't fuck with the magic.*

One day, after a lovely session of morning lovemaking, lying in each other's arms, Peter mused that he would like a child with Beverly. *Yes* was all she could say. *Yes. Yes, Peter. For you, Peter, all is yes.*

Beverly went to the bathroom to wash up and throw away her diaphragm when it seized her. She wasn't sure that she could share Peter. Not with anyone, including a child of their making. This thought made her feel horrible. The guilt was crushing. Beverly had been able to tell Peter absolutely everything, but she could never tell him this.

She threw the diaphragm and spermicidal gel into the trash.

*

The pregnancy was rather mild when compared to other mommies she encountered during it. For nine months, Beverly rubbed her swelling belly, carrying what she thought of as *Peter's Present.*

They gave birth to a child so angelic, she made Shirley Temple look like a catcher's mitt. Peter taught her to speak perfect English, skipping any baby talk phase altogether.

All of this, the flood of memory, was drowning Beverly. She couldn't take it. Not now.

She fled upstairs and took a Xanax to bed.

Perhaps tomorrow. Tomorrow would be a good day. A good day to die.

Chapter 7 - Babysitting

It was Friday night. Digger's orange VW bus pulled up to his mother's friend Monica's duplex and parked on the street. He'd be babysitting her two small children, Simon and Simone, ages seven and nine. The still Winter air was biting with cold. Digger trotted up the steps and rang the bell.

She was going on a date. Monica looked like Morgan Fairchild, but with frizzy hair. She was thin and wore thick eyeliner.

The low ceiling made Digger feel quite tall. He stood while being briefed.

"No scary movies," Monica instructed Digger while putting in an earring. "It gives them nightmares. And, I want 'em in bed by eight."

"Copy that."

Monica gave herself a quick pat down.

"Keys, purse, cigarettes. Check."

She kissed her kids goodbye, a peck on the lips each. This always gave Digger the yucks, people kissing blood relatives on the lips.

"Okay, kids! Mom's gone! It's party time!" announced Digger. The kids squealed.

Simon and Simone loved Digger. Unlike their other babysitters, Digger didn't just invite boyfriends over, ignore them, and eat all of their ice cream.

Digger let the kids play with their toys in the living room with the TV on. Usually, toys were confined to their bedroom. They played a board game called "Trouble." Simon pressed the plastic bubble in the middle of the board, and it popped, causing the die inside it to tumble and give a different number on top.

"Oh, man! Simon's gonna win!" moaned Simone.

"I wish that you were our dad," said Simon, moving his game piece six places.

"Yeah, you could be our dad… or boyfriend!" This made Simone fall on her side with laughter. She was covering her mouth with her hands.

"Me?!" Digger exclaimed comically. "I'm too old to be your boyfriend!"

"No, you're not!" yelled Simone. Simon joined, and they both began to chant.

"No, you're not! No, you're not!"

Then Simon broke off.

"You know what you are, Digger?"

"No!"

"You're a dopey taco head!"

Apparently, Simon could not have said anything funnier because Simone nearly turned blue, chanting, "Dopey taco head!" She rolled around the floor, yelling, "Dopey taco head!"

"What do ya say? Is it time for art class?" Digger baited.

The siblings erupted in a very loud *yeay*!

They had "art class," making glorious fiascos with markers and crayons.

When 8 o'clock rolled around, they begged Digger to stay up. Their saying *please* sounded like a bicycle tire going 'round with a leak in it.

"Okay, but just until 8:30. And don't tell your mom."

They watched "Silver Spoons" on TV.

Digger didn't even pull the curfew on them when the clock neared 9:00. The kids were so drowsy that they just fell asleep in front of the TV. Digger scooped them up, one at a time, and carried them to bed.

With the place basically to himself, Digger turned off the TV and took advantage of Monica's record collection.

With Paul Simon's *Mother and Child Reunio*n on the turntable and the lights down low, Digger sat on the living room floor and sketched on the coffee table. He drew figures from his imagination, handsome men in crisp shirts and trousers from the 30s, and women with necks like swans.

Monica staggered in sometime after 11:00.

"How was your date?" Digger heaved himself up onto the sofa.

"A bust." Monica flopped on the sofa, next to where Digger now sat. "All this guy did was talk about himself. Didn't ask me *one thing* about me."

"Sorry to hear that."

"*And,* he was going bald. The food was good, though. You want some leftover lobster?" Monica held up a swan made of aluminum foil.

"Nah, I'm good."

"Let's check on the kids."

Digger followed Monica to the bedroom that the two kids shared.

The kids snored softly, one lying on his side, the other on her back.

Monica tiptoed to their beds and gave each a kiss on the forehead or cheek.

She then closed the door, latching it shut. This surprised Digger, who expected her to leave it open a crack, as he thought was customary for kids that age.

Monica spun around and caught Digger in a kiss. He didn't pull away, although the thought did run through his mind. She tasted like cigarettes and Mai Tais.

This was his mother's *friend*. How could he do this with his mother's *friend*? This kiss swelled into a full-blown grope session, with tongues included.

Digger followed her into her bedroom. He loved older women. They *knew* stuff.

Afterward, Monica stuffed a small wad of bills in Digger's pants pocket, and he went home, not sure if he wanted this to happen again. Take *that*, mom.

Chapter 8 - I Don't Like Your Surprises

Sunday. A day of rest. A day to catch up on sleep.

No dice.

"Get up, lazy bones! It's almost noon!" Digger's mother yanked the blankets off him.

"Mom! I work sixty hours a week in a factory, plus school!"

"Yeah. *Night classes*," she sneered. "Well, you're not gonna sleep all day. I need your help."

"I was going to work today."

"Work? The factory is closed on Sunday."

"Work on my drawing." Digger jabbed a thumb in the direction of the drawing-in-progress on his art table.

"Oh, *that*. You can have fun after you've done your work."

Digger got in his mother's glossy car and she drove him about five miles away, to a vacant lot. A property Digger's mother had listed was nipple high in weeds and brush, and she wanted it cleared to increase its chances of sale. He got out and surveyed the drybrush that obscured everything else.

"Seriously?" he asked, bewildered. Digger just stood there with work gloves, shears, and a hoe. It was a commercial lot. It was huge. "You have *got* to be kidding. This'll take *days*."

"Oh, quit yer bitchin'," she shouted through the open window on the passenger side of her slick real-estate-mobile. "You'll have plenty of time to play art later. This shouldn't take you more than a couple of hours. Call your friend Kevin. He can help you. I have a surprise for the two of you when you're done!"

There was no way in hell Digger was going to call Kevin for help. Kevin had said, on more than one occasion, "I don't like your mom's surprises." Plus, Digger was embarrassed that he was so powerless when it came to his mother.

"I'll take you to a movie when I get back," Mom promised.

"I don't want to go to a movie."

"There's that attitude again."

Mother pulled away, leaving Digger there alone among the weeds and rocks.

Digger looked all around him. He had no idea where to begin. Ultimately, he figured, just start anywhere.

He tried to hoe out the larger brush. Man! The dirt was rock hard. He bent over and pulled, so as to stretch, but not strain his lower back muscles. Even in the wintertime, Digger wished he had brought a hat, for he was soon dripping with sweat.

As the time dragged, Digger began to mumble to himself. *Fuckin' bitch. I hate that fuckin' bitch… I'll show her. Just you wait…*

He tried to fantasize about splitting his mother's skull with the hoe, but even in his fantasy life, he couldn't do it. She just laughed at him. He would take swing after swing, but no goin'. He couldn't connect, let alone harm her with a blow.

She thought he was an idiot. That was clear. She saw him as the afterimage of his father. That was not a good thing.

Some of the trash bags ripped and tore where the twigs and branches poked through.

Digger dragged them into piles as the lot showed more and more dirt. He wiped his slick forehead with his arm. His sneakers and pants were covered in painful burrs.

*

The sun had long gone by the time his mother returned. Digger stood beneath a flickering streetlight in the cold. She pulled up smoothly, bearing burritos from La Flor de Mexico, his favorite Mexican place. The entire lot had been cleared and gathered into large, neat piles and stacks of green plastic bags.

"Looks fantastic! Good job! Get in. We'll catch a movie. I got the movie section." Mother wasn't wearing what she had been earlier in the day. She'd taken herself a shower. She'd changed into clean clothes. She looked refreshed, like she'd had one of her trademark siestas. Digger was disgusted with her.

Digger took his foil-wrapped chile verde burrito from her, without entering the vehicle.

"I'm gonna walk home," said Digger. "If you don't mind."

His mother made that face, the face she made whenever he or his sister Audrey brought up the subject of their father.

"Suit yourself." With that, mother peeled out, fishtailing slightly as her car shrank into the distance.

Digger hoofed it the few miles home, where he took the greatest shower of recent memory. He then plowed his face into the pillow, where it stayed until 5:30 the following morning.

*

There was no mercy in an alarm clock. It sprang to life, buzzing like the wrong answer on a game show. It was time to get up for work. A good night's sleep after a hard day's work. Nothing like it. His mind felt cleansed and free, like after a long, good cry.

Digger grabbed a couple of strawberry Pop-Tarts from the kitchen and headed out the door, lest he be roped into any more of his mother's nonsense, although that was unlikely. She wouldn't rise for many hours.

He rubbed his hands together, then jammed them into the pockets of his jacket while his VW bus warmed up.

He finally pulled away and toward the freeway. He tried to merge onto the onramp, and a small truck let him in.

This was the time of day when all of the sane people were on the road, the people who didn't cut you off like maniacs, not the broken ant farm of nine-to-five-ers, leaning on their horns and slamming on their brakes. No. Rush hour was for your garden variety psychos.

*

Today, the balloon factory work felt especially good. Digger could work up an honest, clean sweat and let his mind wander or just marinate. He was grateful to be hoisting and hauling, heaving and stacking. He felt very connected to his body, which wasn't his usual state. It gave his mind a chance to breathe.

Digger knew that he needed out. He had no idea how, but he was going to get away from that mother of his, if it killed him.

Chapter 9 - Intro to Print Illustration

Tonight was the first meeting of the Tuesday-Thursday night Intro to Print Illustration class at Design Center. Digger sat himself down in the second row. Not too close, not too far. He was excited but trying to play it just a little cool.

The upstairs classroom was a sterile environment of white walls, fluorescent lights, crit rails for displaying student work as it was being critiqued, and concrete floors, with long, sturdy tables and square metal stools.

Students trickled in. Some had been there early.

Dean was killing time before the teacher got there by showing off his big, bulky student portfolio to the oohs, ahs, and silent assessments of a few of his fellow classmates. No one else had brought their "books" to class.

The first of Dean's pieces was a graphite rendering that depicted a large face being pulled in all directions by fish hooks that pierce the skin. The face appeared to be Dean's. A tortured self-portrait.

He then showed a charcoal drawing of what appeared to be himself, nailed to a crucifix. There were images of nude female bodies and hooded barbarian executioners. All showed shaky draughtsmanship and a muddy sense of color, Digger thought. He was just okay.

"My! You are such a talent! I would love to buy you coffee and pick your brain!" Jean, a painfully needy woman in her fifties with a bowl haircut, fawned over Dean. Digger had overheard Jean talking before the start of class. She had recently divorced, and this was "her time."

"That shouldn't take long," muttered Digger.

Jean heard this and shot Digger a look.

Don, the teacher, entered, and all eventually went quiet.

"Okay, class. As most of you already know, I'm Don O'Conner, Assistant Dept. Chair of the Illustration Dept. at Design Center. And this is Intro to Print Illustration. Nighttime students, you have the option of taking this class, Pass or Fail, in place of a letter grade. Full-timers have to take a letter grade." Don had a mimically nasal voice and nostrils that gave him the appearance of a permanent sneer.

Various grunts and groans of displeasure rippled through the room. The day students sneered at the cluster of night students. One whispered something into the ear of another and laughed.

"You don't get grades in the real world," said a disembodied voice.

"The hell you don't," Don snapped. "In the real world, you are *constantly* being graded by your boss, your client, your spouse... the *IRS*, the *DMV*. Even more so for freelancers. Every day, you gotta prove yourself. Every job is a first impression."

The class sat rustling.

"Okay, class," Don said, trying to restore order. "Let's get started now. Just what is illustration, anyway? Show of hands."

Several hands went up, roughly a third of the class.

"A picture you see in a magazine, or a movie poster, maybe?" postulated Jean.

"Illustration is the art of bringing a story to life," Dean explained with exasperation. Several students nodded, *Sounds good to me.*

"Illustration isn't Art," said one from the group. The noise level rose with the argument.

"Settle down. Settle down," Don began. "Illustration exists to support a text. It does not stand alone. It's an extension of an essay, a chapter, a magazine article... It's usually meant for reproduction, so if it doesn't print, it doesn't count. I've prepared a slide show. Lights?"

On Don's cue, the lights went down and an image of a J.C. Leyendecker Saturday Evening Post cover was suddenly projected on the erased-empty, white marker board. Digger was enthralled. He didn't want the slide to change, ever.

Hair slicked back, wearing a stiff shirt with a high collar, the Arrow Shirt man who was projected on the wall *was* stylish, and J.C. Leyendecker was style's king.

"In the old days, there was an emphasis on traditional drawing and painting, but, partially due to the influence of photography, luckily, we've evolved beyond that now." Don continued. "What I guess we used to call classical drawing and composition reads now as, I dunno ... hokey."

The image changed to one of a more "current" illustration. It showed a roughly cut-out, low-res Xerox of a businessman figure with a briefcase, a cut-out of an airplane, and a cut-out of a telephone, all glued to a global map. They were connected by curved, dotted lines. The word "synergy" was stenciled across the bottom.

"This is one of mine. It's for Business Journal Weekly. You see how text is integrated and how image becomes a textual element."

Dean just had to speak out. He'd *had* it.

"Wait a minute," Dean said, loudly, clearly. "Nobody has moved beyond drawing and painting. That's just one style."

"Well, maybe *you* haven't moved on…" kidded Don. Snarky laughter. Digger does not laugh.

"A style not everybody cares for," argued Dean.

Jean raised her hand. "So, you're saying that drawing and painting are outdated?"

"As we think of it," answered Don, "Yes."

After the slide show, they all took a coffee break. Upon returning, Don took his place in the front of the classroom, standing at the crit rail. On the rail was a record album, a CD, and a cassette. It was Sting's *Dream of the Blue Turtles.*

"Alright. Back to business," commenced Don. "First assignment is an album cover. We're lucky enough to get a friend of mine from A&M to come in as a guest Art Director to judge. It's the new one by Sting."

A mixed reaction rippled through the class. Don continued.

"Go out and get the record. Record, tape, whatever. Listen to it. Next class meeting, I want to see sketches, three different ideas, minimum. The week after next, our guest will be in to critique the final pieces. And don't forget to pick up your supply lists." Don pointed to a stack of papers on the table in front of him.

"Okay. Class dismissed. See you all Thursday."

*

The living room was dark, except for what light bled from Digger's sister's bedroom. He turned on the living room lights.

Large sheets of newsprint were taped to the walls. They read, "I AM A POWERFUL, BEAUTIFUL WOMAN," "I FORGIVE THEM," "I AM THROUGH PRETENDING TO BE HELPLESS," and "I WILL NOT LET OTHERS OBSTRUCT MY JOYFULNESS," in thick Marks-A-Lot Marker.

Digger's sister Audrey, a twenty-two-year-old, seemingly uninfected by any sort of enthusiasm, entered from her bedroom, having heard Digger's entrance. She had straight, jet-black hair with bangs cut straight across. She had what many called "resting bitch face."

"Mom's doing another seminar. See?" Audrey pointed to the sheets of paper on the walls. "Affirmation contracts. She'll be gone all weekend."

"I had wondered why the house had been so quiet."

"Mom says, don't forget to take out the garbage."

Without another word, Audrey turned her back and closed her bedroom door behind her. From behind the door, a stereo clicked on.

Digger dragged the heavy trash cans to the curb. He removed the folded envelope from his pocket. It had the directions to haircutter Bridget's house. Boy, could he use a birthday party.

*

Audrey closed a BAM magazine and flipped through a Circus magazine, lying on her bed. She had to be at work at Cards Okay! at nine in the morning to open up, even though the mall it was in didn't really open for business until ten. Her gig at Cards Okay! was one of her two jobs. She also worked at Hot Dog on a Stick. She felt the uniform alone justified her shitty attitude.

Audrey was saving every cent to, one day, blow this "bone-dry, dead-ass town." She didn't even pay for the magazines. Jane, her manager and kinda friend, had been done with them and left them in the employee lounge.

The Ramones' *Sheena is a Punk Rocker* shouted out of her portable radio/cassette player.

She was three years older than her brother Digger.

Digger. That dumb ass. He may be able to tell you the square root of the French Revolution, but he's still a dumb ass.

People were always taking advantage of him. Sucker. No wonder Mom had no respect for him.

The phone rang. *Who would be calling this late?*

She picked up the receiver.

"No, Kevin. Digger's not here," lied Audrey. "How I'm doing is none of your business. I'm not his secretary, so no, I won't give him a message."

Audrey hung up and returned to her thoughts. *Who could respect Digger? He's harmless. He's worse than harmless. All he does is make his stupid little drawings. He's a coward, no killer instinct.*

Chapter 10 - Bridget's Party

A few nights later, Digger pulled up to the curb and double checked the address written on the scrap of paper envelope.

There were a few young adults smoking on the front lawn. Loud music pulsed through the neighborhood. The front door was wide open, so he walked right in.

It was a two-story house, completely dark but for a few colored light bulbs. The music of The Cramps thumped through the walls.

Some bodies were dancing. Some were draped across sofas and stairs. The smoke of pot and cigarettes hung and swirled in the air. Digger tried to blend in, but seemed still to stick out, as if all moved in dreamy slow-motion but he.

He pushed through the bodies, looking for Bridget, until he was blocked by a shapely brunette who lassoed him into a tight and slinky dance.

To Digger, she was an exotic older woman. He tried not to grin like an idiot or paw like a puppy. He swiveled and swayed with her until he heard Bridget's voice.

"There you are! You made it!"

"Here. I brought you this." Digger handed her a tin of Almond Roca with a handmade card. The card was watercolor on the front. Inside, he had written something innocuous. After all, he'd met her only once.

Bridget pulled Digger into the downstairs bathroom. They faced each other in darkness. Her breath smelled of wine.

"You like my friend."

"I like you."

Bridget kissed him hard. They groped and grappled. They investigated each other's tongues. Digger reached into her bra and grabbed a supple handful. She rubbed him on the crotch like she was starting a fire.

Bridget led him up the stairs by the hand.

She locked the bedroom door as the party continued downstairs.

Digger lay upon her bed, on his back. She jerked her head, indicating the record player.

"Put something on."

She disappeared into the adjoining bathroom. On the wall hung a poster of *A Chorus Line*. Next to it, a travel poster of Spain, surrounded by thumb-tacked vacation snapshots.

Digger ran his fingers through the stacks of LPs that leaned against the wall and chose Al Stewart's *Time Passages*.

He dropped the needle on the spinning record, then rolled onto his back, shimmying off whatever was left of his clothing.

Bridget re-entered the room in a dressing gown.

It dropped from her shoulders, revealing a nude, towering civilization of hips, shoulders, and breasts. She bore a bottle of Rose Milk lotion in her right hand, and she dropped to her knees.

Digger's eyes fluttered as Bridget took him into her mouth.

She crawled up into bed and they kissed with increasing ferocity. They nibbled and bit. They locked hands and flexed against each other.

Their play got a little rougher. Bridget could sense Digger holding back.

He had her breast in his mouth when she urged him.

"Go on. Bite," she instructed. Digger bit. With Bridget's hand clutching him ever tighter, he bit harder.

"Do it," she said. "Do everything."

When they were spent, Digger rolled off of her.

"Happy Birthday," Digger wished Bridget.

"Yeah. Happy Birthday to me," she smiled.

The next morning was overcast. It could have been just about any hour. Bridget got up and dressed. Digger took the cue and followed suit. They went downstairs, and Bridget took a look at the kitchen. It looked as though a dump truck had left a load of dirty dishes in the middle of the room.

Bridget chose to be distant rather than awkward. She spoke to Digger without looking at him.

"You want breakfast?"

Bridget and Digger plowed into their eggs and bacon at a local coffee shop.

"Ugh. I hope you don't mind eating here. The house looks like a bomb hit it, and I'm not up to dealing with it just yet."

Bridget took a peek under her bra.

"Jesus, kid. You sure got a trick or two up your sleeve."

She gave Digger a peek. "Look. Black and blue."

Digger didn't know what to say. He finally came up with "You're welcome!"

Bridget's attention drifted out the window. She grew quiet.

"Spain, huh?" asked Digger. "I saw your poster."

She took in a big breath, then let it out.

"I went this past Summer," she said wistfully.

Bridget's eyes remained fixed out the window.

"Glad I did it. Really glad. Probably won't have the courage or opportunity again. Not to mention the money." Bridget continued to stare out the window. Digger wondered again whether or not to mention the Study Abroad program the junior college was offering. Digger knew he wasn't going himself, so why bring it up?

This whole experience was strange and new. Digger didn't have all that much experience in the arena of sex to begin with. He had very little to compare his own experience to. His first time was at a party with a girl who couldn't remember his name. Romance didn't even figure into the equation.

"Ah. Spain. Spain Spain Spain. Without money, we're all just slaves. We're stuck here. Me. You. All of us. Shit town."

Digger said nothing. Bridget was beautiful, staring at something lost in the ether. She finally broke her spell.

"So, you want to catch a movie or something? I could go down on you in the theater."

"I can't. I gotta buy stuff for a class."

"For a class," Bridget nodded. "This class must be pretty important."

Digger felt that he might have insulted Bridget. But now that he'd tripped that wire, he had no idea how to back out of the trap.

He picked up the check, wished Bridget another Happy Birthday, and they headed out of the diner. She drove Digger back to his car.

Bridget's words lived for Digger, and right now, escaping the slavery of always being broke trumped the greatest balcony blow job.

Chapter 11- Treasures, Old and New

Dusty windows were papered over with yellowing hand-lettered signs, advertising "DRAFTING SUPPLIES!" and "BIG BARGAINS!" The storefront sign read, "BECK'S ART SUPPLY STORE."

From the outside, you wouldn't know the place was still in business.

Armed with the list of required materials for his Intro to Print class and a modest wallet, Digger slowly treaded the aisles.

This place had cheap, if ancient, backstock. Bottles of ink that looked like they dated back to the '50s. Pads of tracing paper that yellowed at the edge. Digger was giddy.

"Cool," He purred to himself.

The elderly proprietor emerged, summoned by the door dingle.

"Only the best!" the owner shouted. "Real rabbit gesso. Not that synthetic stuff. We got Benzyne. Anything you need."

"Doesn't Benzyne cause damage to the nervous system?" asked Digger. The proprietor shrugged. Digger had learned at the junior college that Benzyne attacked the nervous system through the skin. It was a painfully slow and torturously irreversible experience. He'd often fantasized about pickling his mother in a barrel of it.

"I'm no doctor," quipped the proprietor.

Digger worked through a huge pile of ancient, oversized books. Their endpapers were browned and brittle.

"Wow. Look at these endpapers. Like pirate treasure maps!" said Digger

"Treasure is right! Look at those books. Pure gems. One dollar each!"

Digger picked up an expensive sable brush and consulted the price tag. Sable. For laying pure black India Ink, there was nothing better.

He glanced up at the proprietor at the register on the far end of the store. He then returned it to its place on the shelf. Not now.

Digger made his way to the register and paid for his items before heaving his haul to his VW Bus. He consulted his list. He had an album to buy.

The door made an electric *bing-bong* as Digger entered the record store. There were hanging mobiles made of flats, thin cardboard promotional posters that looked just like the record covers, rows and rows of LPs, and walls just plastered with oversized posters. Midnight Oil's *Beds Are Burning* thundered through the speakers.

I could spend all day here.

First, he went to the wall where they displayed the posters for sale. The display opened like a huge book mounted on the wall. You turned each large, thick, stiff-framed double-sided page that showed off the variety of posters the store offered. The actual posters for purchase were rolled and wrapped in plastic in a wire bin below the display. There were The Doors, Duran Duran, Bob Marley, and Menudo.

Rows and rows of vinyl records, stored in neat bins, were separated and classified by plastic dividers. He went to the Pop/Rock section. He thumbed through the As: Abba, Adam and the Ants, Alphaville, Animotion... the Ss; SteelyDan, The Smiths... down to the end of the alphabet, XTC, Frank Zappa... He could spend paycheck after paycheck on these things. Don't even *start* him on the 45s.

Another wall was dedicated to accessories–record spacers, record brushes, record sleeves...

Digger's inner nag told him to wrap it up and get back to business. He had shit to do and a short time to do it. He made his way to the cash register.

"I'm looking for a copy of the new Sting album, *Dream of the Blue Turtles*. The guy behind the counter pointed to a wall display of recent releases.

"You want the LP, tape, or CD?"

Digger spent a lot of time driving from Point A to Point B, so...

"I'll take the cassette."

"That'll be $7.99, plus tax." Digger wished he could stay, wished he had more money, *lots* of money. Digger's sketchbook lay on the counter as he paid in crumpled cash.

A grin spread across Digger's face. It was time, time to show the world what he was made of. Those kids in his illustration class were expecting mere homework from a mere student. Well, they had another thing comin'. He was gonna bring something... killer.

Chapter 12 - Little Brown Bottles

Beverly lugged a bottle of wine up the pathway to her best friend, Patsy's place.

Patsy had a guest house behind the main house. She loved her place. Her rent had been the same for ten odd years, so she was staying put. Red violet bougainvillea clung to the wall surrounding the front door.

Patsy was making lunch for the two of them. Probably sandwiches, Beverly thought, as that was pretty much the limit of her culinary repertoire.

"Come in!" yelled Patsy from inside, as Beverly neared the door.

Standing in the kitchen, the two women sipped at their pear wine while Patsy sliced a ciabatta ham and turkey sandwich on the bias.

"So, how you holdin' up? You been sleepin'?" Patsy wasn't much for chit-chat. She got right down to business. Patsy had bad skin that made her resemble a nectarine.

"Patsy, if life were a gym, I'd just stop paying the dues."

"Uh huh." Patsy leaned both fists on the countertop and placed a great deal of her weight on them. She tried to be delicate, but Beverly knew that really wasn't her.

"I miss 'em too," she said.

Patsy took a small brown bottle from her khaki shorts pocket and placed it on the counter.

"So, that's it, huh?" asked Beverly.

"That's it."

Beverly held it in her palm before holding it up to the light.

"Cyanide?"

"Can't tell you that." Patsy sipped her wine.

"Where did you get—"

"Can't tell you that, either."

Patsy slid Beverly her half of the sandwich and motioned for Beverly to follow her to the patio chairs on the side of the little cottage.

"Patsy, I'm so sorry that you're involved in any of this," said Beverly, holding her sandwich. One of her many guilts was that she was still eating as though nothing were out of the ordinary. She thought that she should be rightly repulsed by food, that she should be as thin as a rail.

But, here she was, as if she were an animatron from Country Bear Jamboree, programmed to perform the same repetitive tasks, without deviation, just ready to hoist food to her mouth.

"None of my business, really," admitted Patsy with exaggerated neutrality. "I can't imagine what hell it's like for you to even sit here. It's only my own selfishness that made me almost pour that crap down the toilet."

"Oh, bullshit, none of your business." Beverly now referred to the bottle. She placed it in her purse.

"What does it taste like?" she asked with a touch of fear.

Patsy shot Beverly a look that didn't *exactly* call her a dumbass.

"Right." Beverly took a beat. "It's really me who is being selfish, aren't I?"

"Look, as I see it, it's not selfish to be on fire and want to be put out. If you can no longer hold up your end of a piano, you drop it." It was Patsy who seemed to be taking her bites with an uncharacteristic pause, which was surprising because when it came to chowin' down, Patsy held her own with the best of 'em.

"It's your choice, and I'll always back you up, Beverly. You know that."

*

Several years ago, Beverly did some freelance work for a few magazines. One of them was as art director for GolfClub Magazine.

A stout and powerful woman intercepted Beverly after she entered the door.

"I'm Patsy. I run the place," she joked. Patsy had an iron handshake.

"Beverly. My pleasure."

After showing Beverly the copy machine, the coffee machine, and the ladies' room, Patsy took her into an empty office.

"And this is yours."

The room was decorated with T-squares, Pantone swatch books, and tear sheets, pages torn from magazines. There was a standing desk with a swinging arm lamp and a very high stool.

"I feel at home already," Beverly commented with genuine warmth.

"We've got ads to lay out, pronto, and our usual gal is—" Patsy began.

"Went out and got pregnant on me!" Hollis, the boss, blustered in and introduced himself. "But don't look at me. I'm a married man! Call me Hollis. I own this whole operation."

He made some more sexist jokes. Beverly pretended not to hear.

"Nice to meet you, Mr. Hollis," Beverly lied.

"Yeah, we are mighty behind, so we're gonna be playing catch-up 'til we ship this issue." Hollis checked his watch.

"Aw, hell's bells. It's lunch time and I have to run. Just listen to Patsy. She practically runs the place."

He gave Patsy a wink, then disappeared into his office to retrieve his briefcase before leaving the larger offices entirely. Patsy's face held a passive smile.

"Where you parked, Beverly? Hell, we'll take my car."

Patsy drove Beverly to the nearby country club.

"This place has its own members-only golf course. I'll sponsor you, fast-track you to a membership."

"Really? How long does it usually take?"

"Without Hollis' backing us? Shoot. Without Hollis, we may as well be women."

"Ladies, if you'll sign in?" The clean-cut man at reception wore a blazer with a crest.

"You never ask the fellas to sign in. And, besides, who you callin' ladies?" chided Patsy.

The blazer with a haircut was not amused. They signed in.

"So, where are your husbands?" Blazer pressed.

"Breastfeeding our cats," quipped Patsy.

"We're second-class citizens around here," Patsy said to Beverly. "A good old boys' network. Women are not taken seriously." The two were shown to a table.

"You make it sound like Ol' Dixie."

"May as well be 1860."

They sat, ready for lunch. Beverly gasped at the menu. "So expensive!"

Beverly had the club sandwich. Patsy had the patty melt.

When the bill came, Patsy pulled out a platinum corporate credit card.

"Don't thank me. This one's on Hollis."

On the links, Patsy said that working for the Golf Culture was like getting into bed with the Mafia. One did not do it halfway. They shared Patsy's clubs.

"I've never golfed before," admitted Beverly, while Patsy used her golf ball to squash her tee into the grass.

"Aren't you sweet. Honey, everyone who can see you dressed like that knows that you have never golfed before." Patsy told Beverly she had family in law enforcement. She yelled *fore!*, then whacked the ball to Mars.

She was a fierce golfer despite playing the game only occasionally. Beverly lacked the upper-body strength to really be any good, but not Patsy. Patsy could carry a war-wounded Marine back to safety. They only played a few holes.

"Time we headed back. Probably gonna be a late night. You married?'

"Yes."

"You probably better give hubby the old heads up."

Hollis, the boss, had always been a chauvinist, but Patsy had always laughed it off, even joined in the joking sometimes, but ever since Beverly showed up, Hollis had gotten weird and creepy. He was lecherous. Patsy didn't want to leave him alone with Beverly. Luckily, their activity circles didn't intersect all that often, although Patsy did catch him making up excuses to "check in" on Beverly.

One day, Hollis was going out of town. Dallas.

"To drink scotch, play golf, welch out on hookers and b.s. with the boys," said Patsy to the entire room.

While Hollis was away, Beverly was going over a layout with a freelance graphic designer she'd hired. The designer had used a gradation of a deep burgundy for the background, so dark at the bottom that it was almost black. The illustration of the golf club was stunning. The type was a desaturated variety of peaches, purples, and lavenders. Beverly loved it. So much in fact, that she shipped it without running it by anybody.

Patsy later told her that purple and lavender had an iron-clad association with Women's Golf. No respectable golfing man would be caught dead with a club advertised in purple. The sexism was as deep and clear-cut as the division between the Hatfields and the McCoys.

Hollis came back, and when he saw the ad, he threw a volcanic fit. But by then, it was too late. The issue of the magazine had already gone to press.

The ad ran, and the calls and letters flooded the office. *How dare you?* ... and *cancelling my subscription!*

However, Hollis didn't fire anybody. No, he liked to keep people close to keep abusing them. He couldn't control things if they left him.

For the next couple of weeks, things got more and more dicey. Hollis kept calling Beverly into his office for ridiculously transparent reasons. Made no effort to conceal his attempts to look down her blouse. But he crossed a line.

He touched her.

It shook her up. It shook her up but good. She told Patsy.

The next day, Patsy silently goaded Beverly into provoking Hollis, getting him to yammer.

"You really think that was appropriate, Hollis? Grabbing me that way, in a *work environment*?" said Beverly.

"What? Oh, you mean yesterday?" Hollis's stupidity seemed indistinguishable from inebriation. "Oh, hell yes. I'll chase a damn skirt and what of it? I follow the Golden Rule—he who has the gold makes the rules! I grabbed your cooch, and you know, I'll do it again. It's a sweet cooch. I was just being friendly!" His voice dropped a creepy octave. "You know, I can be a very good friend."

From Patsy's pocket, she produced a mini-cassette dictaphone.

"We could sue you, you know," said Patsy, clicking the dictaphone to stop recording. She tossed it to Beverly.

"It's all yours, Beverly. What do you want to do?" asked Patsy, holding her purse.

Hollis went loco.

"Blackmail *me*, you bitches? I'll see that you go to prison!" He was seething.

Beverly held the tape recorder, and Hollis lunged for it, knocking her back onto an office sofa.

Patsy pulled a gun on him.

"Oh, now you've done it," he said. "I could have you both killed."

"First of all, I don't believe that." Patsy stepped nearer to Hollis. "Second of all, you might want to check which one of us is holding the gun here. Thirdly, my family is about two-thirds law enforcement. I don't think I'd see jail long enough to eat a peanut butter and jelly sandwich."

"Your family? They don't scare me," said Hollis. "Not one bit."

"No. But they raised me." Patsy put the barrel of the gun underneath his jaw and cocked it. "And me, you should be plenty scared of."

Beverly left the office for the last time. She made certain to have Patsy's home number when she did.

Patsy wound up quitting the job after giving herself a retroactive raise. Hollis didn't question it. Nor did he question Beverly's invoices when they arrived, along with an attorney's howdy do, all billed at double time. He just paid them.

Yes, Beverly and Patsy had seen a thing or two over their years together. And now, Beverly couldn't see past tomorrow. She had no interest in it.

But now, she did have something of a plan.

Chapter 13 - 'Round the Clock Dini Topp

Dini Topp most always brought her work home with her. In fact, to hear her tell it, she never clocked out. Everything she did, the selecting and nurturing young artists for the rarified air of Design Center, the fundraising, the Sondheim shows… it was all work, her life's work, and she loved her work.

Dini Topp's skin was well-protected by a thick layer of pancake makeup that kept the sun at bay, as well as hats when she went outdoors. *Nobody wears hats anymore. At least, not on the West Coast.* She had blue eyes whose whites were obscured by eyeliner and mascara. Her blonde hair was coarse and brittle, doll's hair.

Dini Topp's condo was all white walls, track lighting, and chrome. There were Robert Longo and Keith Harring originals as well as Rothko prints and framed gallery posters.

"Everything's one thing," she said out loud, softly, rather pleased with herself.

She dimmed the lights with a small remote control.

"What was that?" asked Dean. Dini Topp had nearly forgotten that he was there.

There he stood, so striking, so blond, so well-muscled, so young. The sex was just okay. She still had some teaching to do.

Dean's ponytail was trendy. Dini Topp decided to find it sexy.

Dini Topp ignored him.

"Dean," began Dini Topp. "How would you like to do something for me?"

"What is it?" Dean asked rather eagerly. Dini Topp was connected and was going to help him "get ahead." She was also his older lover. He loved being an ornament on her arm at gallery openings, soirees… He wasn't quite sure if she actually considered him anything like a *partner*.

"How would you like to help me with the new Design Center Summer brochure?" Dini Topp began. "We could use a couple of your pieces? I also thought you might accompany me to a couple of high schools, talk to the youngsters."

Dean came around behind Dini Topp and spoke in her ear, burying his lips in her bottled blonde hair, clearly overplaying his boy toy position.

"Why, I think I would love that," he said in a breathy voice.

"What do you think you're doing?" Dini Topp said, pulling away, clearly embarrassing Dean in front of no one. "Fine. Go to your portfolio. Get me five of your best figure drawings and a couple of paintings to choose from."

"Now?"

"Yes, Dean, now. I have a lot to get working on. After you bring me the art, you can go down on me."

Dean left the room to select and retrieve his drawings, and Dini Topp opened a portfolio of various student work from the night classes. There was a graphite rendering of a tennis shoe, a blue sky paperback cover for a Stephen King book, and a couple of figure studies. One of them caught her eye. Really nice. Strong line. Great gesture.

Dini Topp looked for a signature but found none on the front. She turned the drawing over and found a squiggle.

She squinted at it. She couldn't quite make it out. It looked like it said, "Digger."

Chapter 14 - Plagiarism

Beverly woke up in her living room just before noon, but it was after one by the time she actually arose. She'd fallen asleep on the couch again, wearing her husband's old oversized joke sweatshirt. It said, "COLLIGE" across the chest.

There was no point in showering anymore, but she did it anyway.

The auto repair shop smelled of oil and dogs. Beverly liked the industrial feel of the place – the power tools, the pneumatic lifts…

Beverly sat in the main office, awaiting the mechanic's diagnosis. She would have liked to have told him that she was in a hurry, but the truth was, she really had nowhere to be. She flipped through an issue of Condé Nast Traveller. *Condé Nasty*, she thought with a chuckle. The idyllic tropical locales made her wish she were there with Peter. What *didn't* remind her of Peter?

The mechanic returned.

"Yeah. It's leakin' oil, alright. Sure, I can do it, but it doesn't look good. I'd need it for a full day, and we would have to order the part first. You can drive it for now. But, don't wait too long to get that fixed."

That afternoon, Beverly and Digger talked over the coffee break in the cafeteria. The Design Center cafeteria was a sexy, ski lodge affair. At night, its floor-to-ceiling windows were dark, and the room was lit with only soft, warm pin lights overhead. Round tables lay out like lily pads in the vast space.

"What time you got?" asked Digger.

"We still have seven minutes left 'til break's over. You doing the *Paint It Black* Illustration Workshop? Sounds like fun.

"I don't think I'm eligible. I'm just a night student."

Using a ball-point pen, Digger sketched out squares and CD box templates in his sketchbook.

"Digger. That's a strange name."

"Nickname. It's what my mom started calling me. She doesn't call me by my name anymore because I was named after my father."

"Sad. How did you get it?"

"I think it started out about me picking my nose, but now mom always says—Digger mimicked his mother—What's the first thing you do when you realize that you're in a hole? Stop. Digging."

"Ah, a mother's love."

Digger closed his sketchbook and turned his full attention to Beverly.

"So, what about you, Beverly? What's the scoop? What's your story?"

"My husband teaches here, in the Academics Dept., English. He's on sabbatical. You really should apply here, Digger. You belong here. They need you here. Promise me you'll talk to them. Don't drag your feet either. Promise me."

"Alright, alright. I'll do it. Scout's honor."

Beverly took off her sweater, revealing her blouse underneath. Digger tried not to stare directly at her bust.

"Wow. That's nice. Perfect color for you. You look like a Sargent."

"Why, thank you. What a lovely compliment. Momma raised you right." She stood. "Patsy would like you. She's my best friend. She's the kind of friend, if I told her, I gotta bury a body, she'd say, I'll get my shovel."

Some students started getting up and heading out the door in unison. Digger spotted Dean.

"That guy's in my night class," Digger pointed out.

"Him? Rumor has it, he's sleeping with admissions princess, Dini Topless, that he's her Flavor of the Month." Beverly shook her head. "Talk about sleeping your way to the bottom. The rumor is that she slept with the straight half of Andy Warhol's Factory in the late '60s."

Beverly checked her watch. "We'd better get a move on."

Digger walked Beverly to class. "Meet you here after class."

"Sounds good."

The students taped their sketches to the wall, all except Dean, who stood his finished ink drawing on illustration board, along the crit rail.

"Who's ready to present?" asked Don. He looked around the room. "Who goes first? No volunteers? Come on, people. This is part of it. It's not all scribbling in your dungeons. You eventually have to talk to your client."

Finally, Jean stood up. "If it's to be, it's up to me," Jean affirmed out loud. She stood in front of her work to address the class.

She presented a collage, a bunch of cut-up Xeroxes of Sting, musical notes, and instruments with some sloppy, ransom note type glued on, clearly a brown- nosing homage to Don's own work.

"Look like anybody we know?" Dean whispered.

Next, Dean presented his ink drawing. It was an intricate depiction of a tragic figure bound, crucifixion style, to a ship's mast in a storm.

Everybody, including Don and Jean, went ga-ga over it, fawning over Dean. Digger, however, saw something in Dean's piece, something familiar.

"You've really captured the nautical theme of the album! Oh, the power of the composition!" said brown-nosed Jean. Jean shot Digger a look.

Just then, Digger realized where he'd seen that image before. He hopped off his stool and sped out of the room.

"Jealous," spat Jean.

Digger trotted into the school library and zipped through the maze of shelves. He scanned the spines until... Jackpot.

He plucked a copy of Berni Wrightson's Frankenstein off the shelf and showed it to the girl "working" the counter.

"Don O'Connor, Room 103, sent me," said Digger, at a mile a minute, "Says he needs this for class. He says he'll bring it right back. Thanks!"

Digger ran out with the book before she had a chance to respond.

When Digger returned to class, he opened the Wrightson book to the proper page and showed it to Don, the teacher.

Dean's assignment was a direct, line-for-line copy of an illustration from Berni Wrightson's Frankenstein. It was all there, the figure, the pose, even the pen-and-ink drawing technique.

Don studied the two, the original and the copy, side-by-side.

"Okay." Don banged his hands together. "Get to work on your revisions, everybody."

Don beckoned Dean over to him. At the college level, plagiarism was grounds for expulsion, Digger remembered. But this was night school, so who knew?

Later, at the end of class, Digger asked Don what he was going to do about Dean. Don said it was being handled and to essentially butt out—this enraged Digger. Digger just knew that he could never get away with a stunt like that.

After his illustration class was over, Digger found Beverly at her fine art class and walked her to her car in the faculty lot, and waved her goodbye. He noticed a puddle of oil beneath her car.

His mind, however, wouldn't let go of Dean and Don. They made his blood boil. Once again, he was powerless over the situation. He just had to take it.

People like that shouldn't be allowed to live.

Chapter 15 - Sleeping in Cars

It was early the next morning. Digger was finally at the front of the line at the Design Center admissions office counter. He slid his completed paperwork across the smooth counter toward the clerical worker, who had other ideas.

"But, I have an appointment. No. I can't just wait here for one of the counselors to show up. I have a job to get to." Digger had been missing work lately.

"I'm sorry, but one of the counselors is out of town and the other is late back from a lunch," said the clerical worker.

Dini Topp popped her head in from her office. "I'll take him!"

She double snapped her fingers at Digger. "Come on."

Dini Topp had the self-satisfied theatricality of someone pretending not to know of her own surprise party. She was a mover and a shaker, a sagging former cheerleader, now well nearing her forties, used to supplementing her fast talk with a little bosomy bounce. Her brittle, yellow hair had been ravaged by chemicals. She spoke without looking at Digger.

"Dini Topp," she introduced.

"Uh. Hello. Very pleased to meet you. People call me Digger."

"Digger. Good name. Good name for an artist."

Dini Topp sifted through the loose drawings that comprised Digger's portfolio.

"Nice line. Very confident. Yes, we could teach you a lot. How long have you wanted to be an illustrator?"

"I don't really know that I do. I just know that I like to draw."

"The fall term starts in September, but I think you should start this Summer. It's easier to get in for Summer."

"But, I don't have a dime. I grew up on food stamps. I shouldn't even be in here."

"What about your folks?" asked Dini Topp.

"Not really an option."

"I like you. You've got a good story."

"Look. I've got no money. I could never swing coming here."

"Design Center usually doesn't give scholarships. To say they're rare is something of an understatement, but if they exist at all, it's for someone like you, and if anyone's gonna get you one ... it's gonna be me." She then sounded like a salesperson. "Digger, how would you like to go to some of the high schools, talk to the kids about Design Center?"

"This is all going a bit fast."

Dini Topp flipped through Digger's sketchbooks. Scenes of elaborate medieval torture devices and flayed bodies filled many pages.

"Digger, you are one naughty boy."

"Those studies are purely academic."

"Purely academic. Love it." She mused over his doodles, then turned her attention back to Digger.

"You have Intro to Print on Tuesdays and Thursdays. Take my class on Mondays and Wednesdays. That'll transfer over. You'll be late, but I'll help you catch up. Then, you won't have to take it when you start in the Summer."

"This Summer? Your class? You teach?"

"Post-Modern Art History. You probably don't know that I spent some time at the Factory when I was younger."

"The Factory? Like Andy Warhol?" Digger pretended not to know this.

Dini Topp threw back her head.

"Oh, the days! You're doing the *Paint It Black* Workshop, aren't you?

"I didn't think I was eligible."

In a brief flurry, Dini Topp stepped out of her office and then back in, waving a workshop application.

She swirled her initials on its upper, right corner and handed it to Digger.

"Go fill this out in the hall, right now, and get it into Claire's box, out front. And, make sure you go to the library and pick up the assignment. Make sure you read the whole article."

With that, Dini Topp shooed Digger out of her office.

"And, work on your proportions!"

"*Proportions*?!" Digger wondered if she said that just to have something to say. He knew his proportions were rock solid. Just ask Walt.

*

Digger stopped by the Design Center Library to pick up the *Paint It Black Magazine* Illustration Workshop assignment.

An empirically pretty, but slumping, disgustingly apathetic library girl worked the desk.

The assignment was a stapled sheaf of several papers. Digger flipped through them as he left the counter. There was a news cover story to read, then illustrate. The story was about Live-Aid, a monster music festival that was to raise money for famine relief in Africa. Participants were to create a cover and two "spot" illustrations. Dimensions were laid out.

Digger drove home. On his way through the front door of his house, his mother stopped him with a written phone message. It was from Bridget.

"Who the hell is this?" demanded Digger's mother, waving the small piece of paper.

"A woman who cut my hair, mother."

"What? Did you forget to tip her? Why is she calling you? Oh, never mind. Where are those flyers I asked you to draw for me?"

"On the kitchen table."

Digger's mother went to the table and held up one of the flyers. It depicted the movie creature E.T., with its glowing finger, telling the viewer to *phone Vista Homes*.

"I LOVE it!" She left the kitchen with her ill-gotten gains, with what couldn't be a broader smile. Digger went to the kitchen phone and dialed Bridget's number.

Digger mumbled to himself, "The words you're looking for are, thank you."

Later that night, Bridget stood over Digger's shoulder as he sketched out a costume for her.

"The guy who does costumes for our drama dept. Just... doesn't cut it. His stuff looks like crap, and it strangles my tits." Bridget kept nodding as Digger drew. She grabbed a handful of her hair.

"I can't decide whether to dye my hair or wear a wig. I don't want to dye, but a wig? Under those fucking hot lights? This is my last play, though, as an actress anyway. Crew work's more fun, building sets, dressing the cast—"

Bridget gestured silent suggestions with her hand as Digger drew.

"Yeah. That's it," said Bridget, smiling at the completed designs. "Looks good. That'll work."

Bridget pulled the straps down of her dress, exposing her industrial-strength bra.

"Okay, Big Boy. Drop 'em."

She tossed Digger onto his back, onto the bed, and blew him. Damn, she knew what she was doing, too.

Getting dressed, she noticed the thumbnail sketches and pencil comps taped to the walls.

"What's this? Homework?"

"Glad you asked! That, my dear, is my secret weapon! It's the illustration series that's gonna put me on the map. If I'm the Beatles, then the *Paint It Black* Workshop is my Ed Sullivan."

Bridget studied the illustrations closely.

"I'm impressed. These are lovely. Portraits. I love portraits." She continued to linger over them. "You're the Beatles. Yeah. Yeah. Yeah."

Bridget slung her purse over her shoulder.

"I'd better be hittin' it, slugger. Thanks for the designs."

Mother saw Bridget leave. She confronted Digger.

"Digger. This isn't a goddamned hotel. Did you get your chores done?"

"Yes, I did. And, I know this isn't a hotel. If it was, I wouldn't be doing chores and there'd be better food."

"You'd be paying your rent, smart ass. I've had just about enough of you!"

"And I've had just about enough of this! Enough of being summoned with a bell! I am not a dog!"

"How *dare* you! I taught you how to read by the time you were two years old. By the time you were four, you were reading *Treasure Island* and H.G. Wells! We wouldn't be in this house if it weren't for me. Your idiot father. All he could say was, We can't afford it. We can't afford it!"

Mother punctuated her words with all-out punches, hitting Digger about the head and shoulders.

"If you're so sick of all this," mother continued, "find yourself a better place! I mean it! You have 'til the end of the month!"

Mother balled up her fist, but Digger shoved her away, and she fell against the wall, where she slid theatrically down and onto the floor.

Digger fled the house with a door slam.

*

Digger slept in his car uneasily at the junior college. His face was smeared against the driver's side window. A banging on the window startled him awake. The bright ray of a big flashlight lit up his face.

It was Levi. Digger rolled down the hand-crank window.

"Yessir."

"Hey, man. You know I can't let you sleep here. Go on home." Levi had an old, rolled-up copy of True Crime Magazine sticking out of his pants pocket.

"Can't." Digger stared at his hands gripping the steering wheel.

"Trouble at home," speculated Levi.

"Yes. Sir."

"Oh. I know the name of that tune."

Digger and Levi made the small hike back to the guard shack. They shared a Thermos of coffee, sitting on the curb.

"Oh. I slept in my car. Plenty. Back before my wife disappeared and life got good. Now, I try to be home, in case my boy needs me. Yeah. He's fourteen. Thirteen? No, fourteen. He's fourteen now.

"Just last week, he wanted to join the damn choir. At first, I was all, What the hell? But then, I thought, hell, let the boy sing, you know? But then, I realized. That's more showin' up as a parent at those concerts or recitals or whatever.

"Last time I had to attend one of those, I realized that my security uniform is the nicest clothes I got. I actually went in my uniform pants, shirt, and tie. Don't get me wrong. I like my uniform. That's one of the things I like about my job, but when a man's work clothes are his nicest clothes. Man. That's jacked up. I mean, I'm a grown man." Levi spat into the distance. "Got no nice clothes."

Levi let Digger sleep in the guard shack.

"Just this once, now."

"Thanks, Levi."

"What do a man gotta do to have just a little in this world?"

Chapter 16 - Where Were You Eight Months Ago?

In Digger's Print Illustration class, the students rustled and chatted, waiting for the session to begin. Don, the teacher, took center stage. Along with him was a smartly dressed woman in slacks who looked like she was in her late twenties. She was here to judge the final album cover art for the "blue sky" project, Sting's *Dream of the Blue Turtles*.

The final pieces stood on the crit rail like a police line-up. The class quieted before Don spoke.

"Okay, gang, let's get started. Tonight, we have a special guest to help us judge our final assignments. This is Emily."

Emily gave a little nod.

"She has been responsible for album covers for music's biggest stars, and she's been doing it for, how many years has it been?"

Emily mouthed the words, *Too long*. This got a chuckle from the class.

"Well, I guess I'll let you take it away!" said Don.

"Hi, everybody. I'm Emily, the art director for A&M Records. I'm responsible for pairing the right illustrator or photographer with the right graphic designer for the right music talent. Who knows? I may be working with some of you in the future."

She stuck her hands in her pockets and rocked onto the balls of her feet.

"Let's get started!"

Most of the students had done one illustration, the minimum assignment. Some, like Digger and Dean, did multiples, images for the front and back covers, plus any booklets or inserts that might occur. (Dean, after his flirtation with plagiarism, redid his assignment.)

She stopped in front of a turquoise colored collage. It included a decoupaged photo of Sting, clipped from a magazine cover, and some small foam rubber turtles surrounding it. There was ransom note-type all around, using individual letters the artist had clipped from magazines.

"That's mine," said Jean, uncrossing her arms.

"Wow. That's certainly literal," the art director observed.

"Why, thanks!" said Jean.

Emily stepped and stopped, waving her hand over each square piece of mini art, using words like "clarity," "second read," and "cluttered."

When she got to Digger's work, she asked, "Hey, whose is this?"

Digger raised his hand.

"Where were you eight months ago when I needed you?"

There were a few chuckles around the room. Even Jean joined in, the way a hostage joins in on making a confession tape.

"Great concept. Great technique," the art director continued. "I like the use of color, how you threaded the warms into the cools. You left plenty of breathing room for type. Terrific job."

Digger nodded a silent *thanks*.

When she got to Dean's, he straightened up big and tall. He had painted a muscular male figure, standing atop a mythical flying turtle, all done in blues and greens.

"Ah, a fledgling Boris Vallejo, I see." Emily searched the painting for something else positive or helpful to say. "Not a bad start. Good effort."

Dean was visibly not pleased. He looked at Digger with eyes that shot daggers.

Chapter 17 - Integrity is Everything

Digger walked into his mother's real estate office and got a chilly reception. Silent and unfriendly stares followed him in.

"Uh, hello? I'm here to see my mother." His reputation apparently preceded him.

"We know who you are. She's showing a property. You can wait for her outside," offered Rosemary, although there was plenty of seating and courtesy coffee.

Digger looked at his mother's desk. There was his sister Audrey's high school graduation picture and a few others of Audrey, her senior prom, one of his mother and her best friend Rosemary, which looked like it was taken at a mall Glamour Shots studio, but none of Digger.

He went outside and waited next to his VW bus.

*

When Digger's mother finally made it to the office, forty minutes past the time she told him to meet, she waved goodbye to her clients who blew her kisses as they drove away.

They talked in the parking lot next to her car. She wore an arm sling, though it didn't seem to slow the animation of the "injured" limb. She had told her clients and colleagues how her son had knocked her to the ground during a family argument. There was a fairly uniform consensus that Digger was a piece of shit.

On her realty vest, Mother wore a button reading, "INTEGRITY IS EVERYTHING."

Digger looked across the street.

A truck was parked at a nearby Sip N' Snak gas pump. It bore the AC/DC and Jack Daniel's stickers. Pumping gas was the guy who bloodied Digger's nose and fouled his sketchbook, a couple of weeks earlier.

This gripped Digger by the spine. It tightened his shoulders and shallowed his breathing. He was frozen with fear. His mother's voice snapped him back into the moment.

"What do you say, kiddo? Cease fire?"

"Cease fire. Hey. Would you take a look at these?"

Digger produced some papers and presented them to his mother.

"It's for some loans and grants. All you have to do is sign."

A colleague of my mother's briefly watched them through the window. She gave a sour look and then left.

"And just why should I do this for you?" asked Mother.

"You're kidding, right?"

"I most certainly am not. You are spoiled rotten, negative, and abusive." She raised her arm in its sling for emphasis.

"You have got to be kidding me," Digger lamented. "I've had it. Fuck this. I don't need your help. I'll do it myself."

Digger's mom started hitting him, punching him with each syllable she screamed.

"Fuck this? I am your MOTHER! How DARE you talk to me like that? Fuck this?"

Digger covered up, did not hit back.

"I hate you!" Digger lied.

"Oh yeah? I hate YOU!"

"I KNOW!! I KNOW THAT YOU FUCKING HATE ME!!" Digger yelled. "EVERYBODY KNOWS!! YOU FUCKING HATE ME!!"

This shocked his mother. She burst into tears and stopped striking him.

"You hate my father! And you hate me because he's not around for you to hate!"

She grabbed Digger in an embrace, struggling against his resistance.

"I don't hate you, Digger. I don't."

Digger's breathing finally settled, but the matter didn't.

Digger's mother righted herself, then returned to her office.

Digger climbed into his bus and just sat for a moment before shuddering himself back into the present. He looked at his watch. Nearly four o'clock. He had told Tony he'd come by to check out his studio. Digger closed his eyes and breathed in through his nose, then out through his mouth.

When he calmed down and his shoulders loosened, he consulted his sketchbook for the directions to Tony's house and started the engine. He cried as he drove.

Tony's house was in an upper-class neighborhood just a few minutes down the 210 freeway from the Design Center. Crew-cutted front lawns with drippings and pools of ivy accented the ranch-styled homes. At one of the afternoon workshops, Tony had invited Digger to come check out his studio sometime. He seemed genuinely surprised and delighted when Digger actually made plans to do it. He'd thought that Digger was just being polite.

Digger parked on the street and yanked the parking brake.

The door to the two-car garage was open. Inside, Digger saw Tony painting on a large wooden easel, the kind they had at Design Center. There was also a drum kit, a sizable workbench, and a sweet trolley for housing a bounty of art materials. Canvas tarps covered the concrete floor.

Tony, in his cap and round glasses, gave Digger a smile and a nod of recognition.

"Hey, Digger man," greeted Tony, each of them clasping the opposite hand of the other in a *soul shake*. "You like reggae?"

"Uh, sure."

"Reggae is the best!" Tony said, popping a tape into an expensive boom box. "That and ska."

The chunk-a chunk-a sounds of Peter Tosh then rolled out of the speakers, filling the garage.

"Turn it down, Tony!" yelled a voice from inside the house.

"My folks," Tony explained to Digger. Then, in an exaggerated low tone, "Gotta keep it on the down low or the neighbors complain, y'know?"

Tony picked up one of his paintbrushes and swirled it around in a tin can filled with turps.

"Can't we close the door?" asked Digger.

"Nah. Fumes, man. They'll kill ya. You never paint in oils?

"No. Not yet, I mean," confessed Digger.

"Or, you can go up in flames."

"Well, there's always that."

Tony wiped his brush off with a rag, then used the brush to grab a few colors on the palette and swirl them around into a thick puddle. Digger just stared at the puddle, a thick, multi-colored swirl.

"Isn't that rad?" Tony beamed. "Paint. It doesn't even have to be anything. It doesn't have to be a portrait or a landscape. Paint is just cool to look at. That's what those guys like Jackson Pollock were saying."

"They were?"

"Yeah, man! They were saying, *Paint is cool!*" Tony started to dab and scrub at the canvas in front of him. "So cool for you to come over. I love to see other people's studios, how they lay out their workspaces, how they organize their tools and their art. I just dig it."

"Thanks for inviting me." Digger was giddy. He'd really never interacted with other artists before. He'd, for better or worse, kept his distance from most of the junior college crowd.

For the next fifteen minutes, Tony painted in silence while Digger observed. The painting was one he had started in a composition class. It was a female clothed in a turn-of-the-century outfit, big hat, parasol, and all. It was solid. Fine painting. She looked like an old ad for Coca-Cola.

"What do you think of that blue in the corner. Knock it back?"

"It is a little loud, I think." Digger wasn't sure of his comment. Tony was a Design Center full-timer, after all, and Digger knew that, for all he knew, he knew very little.

117

"Hey, we got lemonade. You want some lemonade?"

"Actually, I am parched. I could really go for some lemonade," Digger smiled.

"Righteous!"

The two went inside to the kitchen, where they stood, opposite each other, leaning on the counters, gulping their lemonades.

"Tony, I got to ask you something."

"Yeah? Shoot."

"Do you really think that you can make a living at this art thing?"

"Ah, man. Don't tell me you been talking to my folks."

"No, no. Not you. Any of us. Do you think it's really possible?"

"If not us, then who? I mean, it's gotta be *somebody,* right?"

"Yeah, but— doesn't it seem like the world is changing, that the opportunities are drying up? I mean, for guys like us?"

"Look, I don't want to think that far ahead. Maybe I won't make art for a living. Who knows? All I know is this is what I should be doing now."

"But, this is all I've got," said Digger.

"No, dude. I'm sure that art isn't all you've got." Digger's concerned face made Tony break into a smile. "Lighten up, man! You're the shit! You'll be fine. Come on." Tony placed his empty glass in the sink. "I gotta get back to my painting."

Digger and Tony said their goodbyes, and Digger headed toward his bus.

Tony seemed set. He was like a cat, bound to land on his feet, with lives to spare, but what about Digger? What would he have to do to be "set?" How far would he go?

Chapter 18 - Fortress Around Your Heart

At his makeshift desk in his bedroom, Digger took out his 10"x10" piece of cold-press illustration board and masked off the edges with drafting tape. He was blank-eyed and still worn out from his tussle with his mother. He was ready for peace and quiet, for something to focus on.

He lined his butcher tray palette with a uniform layer of paper towels, then he grabbed a spray bottle filled with water and wet the layer down until moist. He then pressed a piece of tracing paper on top, pressing it down until even. This would keep the acrylic paints from drying out too quickly.

Although he paid close attention to the demos, painting was still not Digger's first language. He squeezed some thick ropes of paint onto his palette, then used a plastic butter knife to mix, smash, and chop the paint until he produced a glorious swirl of streaked color.

Digger was listening to the Sting album while working on his next assignment, a series of editorial illustrations for a magazine cover article on the Rwandan pogroms. *Fortress Around Your Heart* flowed through his headphones.

Art was not the way to make money. Everybody said that. At least that's what his family said. All they did was mock him when they weren't ignoring him, that is. The whole *starving artist* thing didn't exactly come out of nowhere. Digger just couldn't imagine spending his days doing anything else. He'd made decent pocket money doing portraits while he was in high school, but that was small time. It seemed to him that everyone he met just wanted to take advantage of him. The people who made the real money on art never once had stained fingers. It was an artist's death they were cashing in on.

His small television set sat atop his dresser. On it, California conservative Wally George slung his finger at the camera from behind a desk, seated next to an American flag.

Digger took a large, soft paintbrush and ran a watery wash all across the top of the illustration board. Across, then down, creating a lovely undulating neutral tone that covered every inch fairly evenly.

He leaned over and yelled through his closed door.

"Hey, Audrey! Could I borrow your hairdryer?"

"Stop yelling!"

Digger got up and went to Audrey's room. She was getting ready for work. She handed him her banana-yellow hairdryer with its cord wrapped around the handle.

"You'd better not break it," Audrey said like a playground thug.

"I'm not gonna break it," Digger said like a playground slouch.

Back in his own room, he plugged in the hairdryer and used it to dry the freshly applied wash, using slow repetition, with it set to the next-to-lowest setting.

While the board was drying, Digger "painted" an "X" on the back, using only water. This would help keep the board from buckling too much. He then used transfer paper to get his line drawing down onto the board. His sketches were precise, with perfect planning for the final piece. Some people worked alla prima, attacking the surface with thick paint strokes and no underdrawing.

Not Digger. He really didn't like surprises.

He stayed up painting far into the night, far past the point where his head jerked, trying not to drop, and his eyes begged to slam shut. He was manic. He'd been here before. He'd be here again.

The next day at the balloon factory, amid growling machinery and loud blasts of compressed air, Digger stacked large boxes onto a pallet, then grabbed a clipboard that hung from a nail on the wall to do some scribbling and check some boxes.

Bill walked up about twenty feet from Digger, waving for Digger to follow him.

"Kid," shouted Bill above the ruckus from the "floor," "we need you to help pack. Huge order."

Digger groaned, then followed Bill to a packing station near shipping and receiving.

Digger turned the tape over in the Walkman he wore on his belt before he began counting. He counted small latex balloons and tossed them into the big metal scoop on the scale that rested on the large shop table. When he had counted 100 balloons, he set the scale to zero. Now, whenever the scale read exactly high noon, there were just about exactly 100 balloons in there.

Digger clicked "play," and The Police's *Synchronicity* filled his ears.

Digger emptied the scoop of balloons into a small plastic bag bearing the company's name. He turned his body one-quarter turn and heat-sealed the bag on a small machine, worked by his foot. He tossed the bag into a large cardboard box and hit the clicker-counter.

This is the part of the job he hated most, not that he really *hated* any of it. It was a good workout and left his mind fresh. Well, mostly. He sketched and studied on his breaks.

About an hour and a half later, Gloria yanked on his shirt sleeve. Boy, was she pissed. Bill was by her side.

"Gloria says your count's off."

Gloria started rattling off in Spanish. Digger understood most of it.

She grabbed the headphones off Digger's head and shook them.

"She says you shouldn't be listening to this while you're working," said Bill. "That's why your count's off."

"I wasn't hired to do this shit. I was hired for the darkroom." Digger defended to no avail.

"Well, if you don't stop wearing the Walkman, she's gonna tell the boss."

Digger promised to work without the Walkman.

Man, was this gonna suck.

*

Late that night, Digger read the writings of Marcel Duchamp, the Dada master, alone at Carrows as a cold rain poured. Karen refilled his hot chocolate. He put on the headphones of his cassette Walkman and listened to The Police.

Digger was feeling sorry for himself. He broke his gloom for just a moment for a chuckle at his own expense.

Nothing like realizing that you're a living cliché. The tortured young artist. Boo hoo. Hell, he thought he might as well lean into it. He took some comfort in the words he read.

Duchamp said that he did not work for the masses. He said that he made art for himself and/or an "ideal public" that may not exist for another ten or twenty years.

Digger knew that he was as green as green could be, but he also knew that he was no poseur. He might not be the real deal, but he was no fake. He didn't have the balls to call himself an *artist*. No, he'd have to earn that.

"You okay, darlin'?" Karen asked. "I'm 'bout to take my break."

"Yeah, I'm great, thanks. Is it cool for me to just sit here until you come back from your break?"

"Sure thing, honey. I just gotta close out your check."

"No problem." Digger pulled out his wallet. It was falling apart. Its Velcro made a weak snap as he opened it. He'd gotten that wallet for a previous birthday.

"You know, come to think of it. I'd better be heading out." Digger pulled his jacket on.

"You sure, honey? It's no problem."

"That's okay." Digger left a five and a handful of change for his hot chocolate.

He checked his watch. It was a little after 1 a.m. He still had time to get some painting in.

Chapter 19 - Think Degas

The next morning, Digger blew into his clasped hands for warmth as he left the house for work. January in California was still January, and last night had been particularly cold, causing the frozen grass to crunch beneath his Converse All-Stars. He still had that hollowed-out feeling from painting all night.

His VW bus was parked on the street in front of his house. The windows had a thin layer of ice on them. He opened the door to get the squeegee, only to find something on his driver's seat. It was a flyer folded into fourths. He looked both ways before he opened it. This only surprised Digger so much, for he never locked his car at night.

It was for a community theatre stage production of *Camelot* in Whittier. Bridget's scrawl was evident. It said. "Hope you can make it! Pleeeeaase! -B" It had a smiley face under the "B."

He squeegeed the exterior windows, then got in the cab and laid the flyer flat on the passenger seat. He started the car. The windows fogged up while letting the engine idle.

"Oh, just great."

He used the squeegee to scrape down the inside of the windshield. When he had determined that the bus had warmed up enough, he pulled down the red faders, engaging the bus's pathetic heater.

He turned on the radio and headed toward coffee.

Digger pulled into the Sip n' Snak and made a quick scan for any unfriendly trucks before he hopped out of the car.

He got himself an apple fritter and hot coffee. There was a "HELP WANTED" sign in the window.

*

At the balloon factory, Digger worked through lunch and made sure that the basket with the darkroom orders was empty.

He watched it like a hawk, and the moment an order came in, Digger dropped whatever he was doing and shot the graphic. He didn't want any orders backing up. He figured that way, he could slip out at three o'clock and make the afternoon workshop at the Design Center at four. He had been pulling this more and more. He was tempting fate, and he knew it.

This did not go unnoticed. Shipper Bill's glance was not without meaning. Bill just shook his square, shaved head.

One of the machines went down, and Bill needed Digger's help changing Maricella, its operator, over to another machine. It was already 2:30. *Shit.* An emergency changeover could take up to 45 minutes.

Digger got the silk screens off of Maricella's machine and onto a new one without too much trouble. He wiped his dripping face with a bandana. He checked his watch. 2:50. The real problem was unjamming the old machine and fixing it so that it could go back into production.

The minute they had Maricella's old machine back online, Digger tore out of there, whipping off his apron and clocking out like Fred Flintstone at 3:10. *Shit.*

While the bulk of the room drew this afternoon's model, Digger, Tony, Jonny, and Rachel huddled and squatted around Pashone's easel in the back of the room. Pashone held open a large book on Degas in one hand and wielded in the other hand a charcoal pencil as if it were a rapier.

The pad on the easel gave a visual breakdown of the composition in the book. Pashone would choose a piece of art from the book, a painting or a drawing, then draw a simplified version on the large pad, amplifying the painting's compositional idea, its main point, so to speak.

He had now chosen "Woman Bathing in a Shallow Tub."

"Degas. Look. It's straight against curve. Straight against curve," lectured Pashone. There was more nodding than blinking.

"Look at the curve of the spine," Pashone continued. "Now see how Degas plays that curve against the straights of the limbs. But Degas picks up that curve and mimics it with the rounded edges of the shallow tub. He chooses his theme and he *sticks to it*. Everything should reinforce your theme, that or directly contradict it, thereby heightening your theme by contrast."

The observers scribbled in their sketchbooks, feasting on Pashone's insights until he concluded.

"That's enough for now." And with that, Pashone turned back to his own easel, picked up his Carb Othello pencil, and regarded the model, ready to draw.

The students all broke, like a football huddle, each returning to their easels and horses.

"Now, as you draw your model," Pashone coached, "think Degas."

But the pose was now over. Time for the model's coffee break.

When they returned from break, Digger straddled his horse and grabbed his charcoal pencil. *Degas, Degas... Straight Vs. Curve...* Digger thought to himself. He regarded the model's pose along with their physical circumstances, props, drapery, etc... The model was a fleshy woman who looked to be in her late twenties. Perfect. He scanned and scanned, picking out opportunities to play the straights against the curves. He *scrape, scrape, dragged* his pencil across until it was time to bang in some tone.

Pashone startled him, so silent was his approach. He spoke softly to Digger.

"That's it. You got it. Looks like it was drawn by Degas himself."

Digger did not answer. He knew better. This was a compliment best digested without comment. He looked over his composition with great satisfaction. By George, it *did* look like a genuine Degas.

*

During the evening illustration class, the students quietly worked on their new projects, some wearing headphones. Don walked slowly from one student to the other, silently monitoring their progress. Jean flagged him down for some assistance.

Some scrubbed graphite dust into illustration board, while others developed their ideas by drawing layer upon layer of tracing paper.

Beverly came into the room wearing gloves and a well-worn artist's apron that belonged to the school and approached Digger, who was just about to dump out the dirty water from his painting bucket.

"Well, there's a friendly face!" Beverly said in a hushed tone.

"Hey there. What are you doing here?" Digger asked.

"Oh, we're on break and I thought I'd come and say hi." Beverly turned her attention to Digger's painting.

"How's it coming?"

"Not bad. Not bad." Digger couldn't help but suppress a contagious giggle, like they were getting away with something. Don looked up at them, and they shushed. Beverly looked up at the clock.

"Oh, shoot. I'd better go if I'm gonna grab a coffee before heading back to class. Talk to you later, Kemo Sabe." As she left the room, she waved her fingers without turning around.

Dean slowly made the rounds, quietly handing out flyers. Dean slid a flyer across the table to Digger.

It was an invitation flyer to a party he was throwing. Digger thought at first that it was a mistake or a mean joke. But, it looked as though the opportunity for Dean to show off his expensive Brewery apartment trumped his sense of rivalry. Digger thought it a tad peculiar.

He just *had* to go.

Chapter 20 - Dean's Party

The Brewery Building stood in the L.A. night, lit from below like something from an old monster movie. It contained loft spaces and high-dollar rent for the trendy, well-to-do, artsy types. It was Old-School Industrial, scrubbed and sterilized beyond recognition. It had killer views.

Digger entered Dean's party in his huge, cavern-like studio. Dancing Otter Pops glowed in the black light as Digger peered over the railing at the crowd. There was a band dressed in all black, although there was more standing than dancing.

The balcony was high enough that one could see the cluster of downtown skyscrapers shimmering in the winter night. Digger instantly felt a potent mixture of disgust and envy. He ached to not just have all of these things; the palatial studio, the f-you money—but to be seen as belonging here, not just with his nose pressed up against the bakery window.

Dean's "work" hung on the high concrete walls and rested on heavy-duty easels. There were canvases up to 8 ft in height, many of them images of hellish agony, if a little wobbly in their composition and anatomical accuracy.

Digger made his way to the fully-staffed open bar. They didn't have iced tea, so he opted for a flavored sparkling mineral water. He just stood there for a while, just taking it all in.

He swam through the thick crowd. Although he recognized a couple of people from the afternoon drawing workshop, it was mostly Design Center full-timers, no doubt there for the free booze.

Digger was there for a good twenty minutes before he heard his name yelled above the grinding thump of the music. It was Tony. He was there with Rachel.

Tony waved excitedly for Digger to come and join them. Digger pressed through the party sardines until he reached them.

"Have you seen Jonny?" asked Digger, mouthing the words more than shouting. He had come to see Tony, Rachel and Jonny as a complete set.

"Said he can't make it," yelled Tony. "Can you believe this shit? Rich kid, right?"

"You check out the 'artwork?'" Rachel asked, then made a yikes face.

"He's full-time, right?" shouted Digger.

"Yeah! Think we ought to find him? Say hi?" asked Tony.

"Sounds like a plan!" yelled Digger.

"Okay, I'm in!" shouted Rachel.

The trio slowly made their way around and through the squirming population. There were people on the black leather sofa and chairs, laughing and gesticulating. A young woman was acting out a story concerning one of the Design Center teachers and a student.

They found themselves in the kitchen, where they checked out the contents of Dean's fridge: an acrylic paint palette, covered in Saran Wrap, loads of Kodak film, and batteries. Bottles of India ink. Cases of Coca-Cola and gallons of orange juice, plus assorted student staples like cookies, peanut butter, jelly, and pickles.

"You're not supposed to refrigerate peanut butter," Rachel informed Digger and Tony.

"Oh, shoot. I gotta use the can."

The three of them then set out on a quest to find a bathroom. Every inquiry they made was met with a shake of the head until they saw a line of people upstairs.

They climbed the stairs and joined the line, where they stood for a bit until Rachel shouted, "Are you in line for the restroom?"

"No!" the stranger shouted back.

"Aw, crap!"

Digger spotted another line, across the way on the same floor. They worked their way toward it and had better luck this time.

After Rachel emerged from the restroom, feeling a *whole* lot better, the trio descended the stairs again, where they found Dean, holding court and laughing with his full body convulsing.

His jokes were mean and obscene. He was getting handsy with a couple of young ladies and was a very loud drunk.

Dean produced and waved around a pistol, a .38 Special, shiny as could be. This elicited a collective *whoa* from the crowd. Perhaps he thought this would impress, but many just left the scene immediately. He said it was given to him by his father. This raised a few eyebrows. Dean was letting people hold it.

The three all felt that this was their cue to leave, so they thought they would just thank him for inviting them at school next week.

Digger played with the idea of swiping the gun somehow, just sticking it in his pants. He wished for an opportunity. Digger knew you never knew when a gun might come in handy.

The next day, Digger went into the office at the balloon factory, the only place in the factory with air conditioning. The "girls," as the boss called them, manned the phones as though they were paid to place people on hold.

As usual, the boss pretended not to see Digger.

"It's a three-day workshop, starting Friday. All I need is Friday and Saturday off."

"Can't do it," the boss responded.

"I *never* ask for time off. It's important."

"Can't do it. I got orders. Besides, you been missing a lot of work lately."

"I've had to register for school and stuff," explained Digger, telling mostly the truth. He had also been leaving early to hit the afternoon drawing workshops with Pashone.

"You'd really rather fire me than give me two days off?"

"I'm not firing you. You just quit."

Back at home, Digger burned the midnight oil, working on his Live-Aid illustrations for the *Paint It Black* Workshop in his bedroom.

He sat with his hands on his thighs at his makeshift drafting table. It was a children's dining table, with a piece of sanded plywood on top. A few phone books kept the plywood propped up in the back, so as to give the surface its appropriate slant.

Walt said that ninety percent of painting is staring. *Well*, thought Digger, *I'm living up to* that *rule*.

Digger finally shook himself into the present and set to drawing some head studies of Bob Geldof of the band The Boomtown Rats and Midge Ure of Ultravox, the creators of Live-Aid.

He would do a stylized, atmospheric double portrait of them for the cover. Digger hadn't yet decided what to do for the two interior images, the ones for inside the magazine. Those would be more editorial, more conceptual.

Digger took out a large pad of smooth newsprint paper that was clipped to his Aerolite drawing board and a medium-hard, sharpened charcoal pencil.

He began to lecture to the walls around him as he began to lightly rough in his boxy head shape.

"Right away," Digger addressed to himself, "you want to identify the direction of your light source." He then answered himself with a question. "Why is that?"

"Why, that's because your light source gives you your shadows, gives you all of your surface information. It describes the structure of the nose, in all of its detail."

"Ah, I see. Why drawing? Why not… selling real estate, like your mother?" asked nobody.

"Great question. I draw because every time I have ever quit and tried to do something else, I wind up backing back into drawing. It's the way I think. It's my arena. I don't sell real estate like my mother because I just can't. I'm not a liar."

After banging out nearly forty minutes of head studies, Digger yawned and stretched, then took the cigar box out from under his bed and put it on his bed with his bank book and the coffee can he kept in his bus for petty cash.

He opened the cigar box. It contained loose one-hundred-dollar and twenty-dollar bills, bound by rubber bands. He counted the bills. He counted them again.

Roughly two thousand bucks.

Then, he removed the lid and counted the contents of the coffee can.

$128.78. Hmmm...

The bank book had roughly $800 in it. That made a total of roughly $3000.

He took out a piece of scratch paper and did some quick estimating.

Let's see. Gas and oil. (scribble, scribble) Art supplies. (scribble, scribble) Food. (scribble, scribble) Insurance (scribble, scribble)... Rent (scribble, scribble)

Digger figured that would last him, maybe ... three months, if he was careful.

He had to make something happen. He didn't know what it was, but it had to happen within the next three months.

Chapter 21 - The *Paint It Black Magazine* Illustration Workshop

The Design Center auditorium was packed, and the overflow filled the aisles. There was excitement and tension in the air. Some were here to be judged, others to be discovered.

Harris, a walking relic in his early seventies, looked like something from an EC horror comic. Neither his teeth, nor hair, nor skin looked of any human hue. He walked like a marionette. Harris took the podium and spoke into the mic.

"Welcome. Welcome. Welcome to the *Paint It Black* Illustration Workshop. (applause, a whoop), Three days of seminars, lectures, presentations, and unique opportunities to rub elbows with some of the actual industry professionals with whom you wish to someday work. I am pleased to welcome and present to you, Ted Woodman, Art Director of *Paint It Black Magazine* (applause), Annie Talaski, frequent *Paint It Black* illustrator (more applause), and you all know Mook."

Big cheering. Whooping and hollering. Rock star illustrator Mook took a step forward and waved to the packed auditorium. He was easily one of the most highly sought-after illustrators in print. He did editorial and highly commercial stuff. His work was amazing and distinct. Mook had a head of dark, cacophonous hair, like Billy Squier. In a trademark slump, he waved out to all of his rowdy fans.

"Ted, it's all yours." Harris passed the torch, then hobbled off. Ted took the podium.

"Well, I'm certainly looking forward to it. What a terrific opportunity to see such a pool of young talent. How y'all doin' out there?"

Cheering, hollering.

"As I understand it, there's some kind of reception tonight at … Don's place?"

Standing along the wall, Don nodded.

"I guess I'll see you all there. Now, I'd like you all to get to know *Paint It Black Magazine.*"

The lights dimmed, and a slide went up on a screen that was revealed as the curtains parted.

Ted began his presentation.

"I launched *Paint it Black* in 1966 from my one-bedroom New York apartment with my wife, Denise, as an active voice in the counterculture. Since then, we have discovered the talents of gifted music and film reviewers, prize-winning journalists, and award-winning illustrators and graphic designers. A lot has changed since then, but we like to think that we have kept up with those changes."

The slides clicked and changed. Images shown were photos of young people with hippie moustaches and bell bottoms, sitting crammed in a small room holding meetings, photos of girls making silly faces and peace signs. There was a photo of a beaming young man holding up an early issue of the magazine.

"From the moon landing to Woodstock and Watergate… from the Clash and The Sex Pistols to Madonna and Menudo, *Paint it Black* has had its finger on the pulse of the culture of young America." Slides showed famous *Paint*

It Black images, covers, photos, illustrations… Rock stars, movie stars, politicians, scientists, farmers, newsworthy civilians…

"Over the years, *Paint It Black* has worked with bright young talent like Annie and Mook and now, you!" Big applause.

That night at a gas station, about to fill up on the way to the shindig at Don's house, Digger estimated the money in his coffee can. He was getting low on petty cash and wasn't just concerned. He was rattled. Digger no longer had a job and still had expenses like gas, rent, food, and art materials, let alone any emergencies.

Don's professional studio was also his house. There were high ceilings, metro racks, and frosted glass. His work area looked out over the ground floor.

The new Talking Heads CD, *Little Creatures,* slapped through the speakers. There was finger food and aluminum tubs full of ice, bottled beer, and soda.

It was a big, two-story place with exposed pipes. Students, faculty, and guests flooded the place, spilling out to the patio areas.

Students, eager to "network," hounded and chased the celebrity guests, including Mook, around the party, who finally ditched them.

Annie Talaski was there, looking like she'd really rather go back to the hotel and turn in early. She checked her watch. Her work was lovely. It was often mistaken for an airbrush, but was actually a very delicate watercolor. She was a *Paint It Black* favorite.

Digger ran his eyes along the spines of the art reference books on the shelves, wondering if Don wasn't worried that people wouldn't break or steal his stuff. He plucked one, "The World of Tomorrow."

"Hugh Ferris. Great stuff." It was Mook, standing just over Digger's shoulder.

"Yup." Digger pointed to the speakers mounted in the ceiling. "Man, this is nice. I like Talking Heads."

"Oh, yeah? What's your favorite?" asked Mook.

"Off the top of my head, I'd have to say the first one. Talking Heads '77."

"You're kidding! Not many people would choose that one." Mook looked off into the air, nodding. "Hmmm. Interesting." Mook took a look around.

"Man, I hate these things. Want to get some air?"

Mook and Digger sat in Mook's parked rental Range Rover. Music played on the car stereo. Digger had gotten his cassette organizer case from his car, and they were playing mix tape roulette. They talked about bands and record collecting.

"Man. When I discovered that record, the first one, I thought I was the only one in the world," Digger rhapsodized. "I thought it was mine alone. It didn't grab any of my friends, but man, did I love it. Played it *to death*."

"No way. I know the critics love Marshall Crenshaw, but I never got around to checking him out. I probably should."

"He's the new Buddy Holly! I'll make you a tape."

"For real?" asked Mook with surprising enthusiasm.

"Absolutely. Where should I send it?"

"Send it to the magazine. They'll get it to me. Here's my card."

Digger couldn't believe what he was seeing. Rock star illustrator Mook was giving me his card, a way to contact him.

"Can I call you?"

"Sure!"

They continued hanging out until Mook felt that he was gonna be missed.

"We'd better be heading back in."

Digger had made a new friend. He could not believe his luck.

Chapter 22- The *Paint It Black Magazine* Workshop, Day 2

Room 100 was a vast, airplane hangar of an art space. The partitions and easels had been temporarily relocated and stored. Most of the hundreds of students, but for a few who dragged in chairs, were sitting on the floor or standing in the far back.

Teachers flanked the room, standing along the walls that were absolutely covered with illustrations, pinned or taped up. There were some scuffles earlier, as some folks were moving or covering the work of other students.

Digger had gotten there at 5:30 am just to stake out his claim. Some of the stuff looked pretty tame and forgettable to him. Trendy stuff.

Harris, Dini Topp, Jon, Ted Woodman, Annie Talaski, and Mook stood at the front of the huge room, looking out over the crowd.

"Can you all hear me? I'd prefer not to do this with a mic," Ted began. "Welcome to Day Two of the *Paint It Black* Illustration Workshop. First question."

A young man raised his hand among the eager many.

"Mr. Woodman. What would you tell a young illustrator, just starting out?"

Ted wasted absolutely no time formulating his response.

"Talent does not matter."

Some shook their heads dismissively. Others hung on Ted's next word. Teachers shuffled their feet.

"Return your phone calls. I mean it," Ted demanded, "If you have talent and don't return your calls, I'll never use you. If you have no talent, zero talent, but you work your ass off and have good people skills, you will work. I guarantee it. You might not be rich. You might not be famous, but you will work ... doing what you love. If you're also talented, all the better. But, in the end, talent doesn't matter."

"Talent gets you laid," said another disembodied voice. Scattered laughter.

"What about finding a style? I always hear that you got to find a style to make you stick out," offered a student wearing a sleeveless t-shirt.

"Don't worry so much about forcing yourself into some kind of 'style.' At this stage, all you'll wind up doing is derivative work. Just do good work. Solid work," said Ted. Mook interrupted.

"Stop trying so hard to be special. To find your voice is to find your place in the world. Your style will find you."

Mook turned to the work on the walls. "Okay. Let's see what you got."

Don handed Ted a bottle of water, and they stepped along the walls of illustrations. Ted stopped and pointed.

"Who's this?" asked Ted.

A hand goes up, halfway back. The artwork in question was a portrait of Bob Geldof wearing a halo.

"Trite," concluded Ted.

The crowd rustled. Mook pointed to three different pieces, each depicting Bob Geldof with a halo. "See? See?" observed Ted. "Same exact concept. Trite."

Ted and Don continued, pointing and critiquing.

Only Annie noticed Digger's work at all. She stopped at his series of three illustrations, his triptych. She looked out into the crowd.

"Who's this?" she mouthed to the crowd.

Digger's hand went up, but Annie was dragged back into Ted's monologue and the collective focus of the room without any regard.

Dini Topp asked, "What about those? Those three?" pointing to Dean's pieces. Ted and Mook mumbled something, then quickly moved on.

Selected students woke and straightened as their work was singled out. Some bit their nails. Some sipped from plastic bottles or gigantic cups.

Finally, they broke for lunch. Students got up and stretched before milling out.

*

In the cafeteria, Digger took his tray to a corner table and sat facing the window. He was moping over his experience during the crit. They didn't even really look at his entries. *And I did some solid work*, he thought.

Dean went with Dini Topp and the VIPs to a secluded, roped-off faculty dining area where a buffet spread was laid out. He caught Digger's eye and grinned before disappearing behind the divider.

*

That night, Kevin and Digger met for another late-night Carrows cram session. Karen the Waitress got the order wrong again, but made up for it by bringing them all of the kitchen mistakes; nachos that had forgotten to *hold the cilantro* and salads that didn't have *dressing on the side.*

Digger perused some of Kevin's books: three on roses, a small pile on architecture, and a couple of auto repair manuals. He flipped through them.

"You know anything about cars, Digger?" Kevin joked. He knew that Digger knew zip about cars.

"Not yet,"

"So, how'd that contest go? You famous now?"

"Yep. Drinks for everybody!" Then Digger got serious. "I didn't even place. The top awards went to this shitty photo collage stuff and some Mook rip-off pieces. One guy stapled a rubber glove to a wooden board. It was about AIDS, he said." Digger was dejected at this telling of the tale. "Some scoffed at this, while others nodded, saying, 'Very bold. Very bold.'"

"AIDS? I thought it was supposed to be about Live-Aid," observed Kevin.

Digger shook his head.

"You still seeing the big blonde?" Kevin continued.

"Here and there. Been busy," replied Digger.

"At least *someone's* getting laid," confided Kevin to his beverage. "Oh, yeah. Ms. King says, Hi."

"Ms. King? You went and saw Ms. King without telling me?"

Kevin shrugged. Ms. King was Digger and Kevin's high school art teacher. She was highly influential on Digger and Kevin, especially Digger. They *adored* Ms. King.

Digger felt betrayed, yet at the same time, guilty for not having kept in touch.

"Hey, man. You weren't around. Like you said, you've been busy."

*

Back at home, Digger sat on the floor in his bedroom, staring blankly at his *Paint It Black* Illustrations leaning against his bed. They were failures. He felt like a failure. He felt like a fraud and that he'd been found out. His confidence was crumpling like a soda can.

Digger's sight grew mushy, and he fell asleep slumped on the floor.

The next morning, the phone rang. "Fuck you!" he yelled at the phone in a spasm. Digger got up and went to the kitchen to answer it.

"Hello?" he said into the receiver.

"Digger, it's me, Beverly. Please, tell me that you're free tonight."

Digger let out a sigh. "I'm free."

Digger had no idea what Beverly had in mind, but it was too late now.

He was doing it.

Chapter 23 - Walking the Freeways

Aw, damn. The car wouldn't start. It was still late morning.

Digger popped the gear into neutral and started pushing the VW bus backward. When he got the car rolling, he hopped in and popped the clutch in reverse, and it bucked to life.

I'd better get an alternator.

Digger drove into the area of town that smelled of tire rubber and axle grease. Chain link fences topped with barbed wire ran all along Valley Blvd. Lots were packed with cars, many with their hoods up, some partially covered in blue tarps.

He kept his eyes peeled for the well-hidden, hand-painted sign that read, "Rick's VW Repair." He pulled in.

A mechanic greeted him as he pulled up. "Hey, there."

"Rick here?" Digger asked from the bus.

"Yeah, he's in the back. Pull your car this way. Follow me."

The mechanic looked around as if looking for a place to put Digger's car. He waved Digger forward, then into an empty spot like an air traffic controller.

It was a tight squeeze to climb out through window, but Digger did, then followed the mechanic back to the office. Off to the right, a large, slobbering Rottweiler growled and yipped while chained to a rusting metal pole.

Rick emerged from an empty doorway leading from the car bays into the office. He wore a baseball-style cap with the company name and a well-groomed beard.

"Digger, the man! What can I do you for?"

"Hey Rick, how much would an alternator run me? I think it's the alternator, anyway."

Rick started tapping a ballpoint pen on the counter.

"Hmmm, what year is your bus?"

"1971."

"A '71." Tap, tap, tap. "Shouldn't run you more than a hundred bucks, plus labor. Say, $180-$185, plus tax."

"When could you do it?"

"Looks like Ernesto's wrappin' up that old lady's Karmann Gia. If I order the part right now, we could get started on it," Rick looked at his watch, "after lunch."

"Yes! Yes! Oh, that would be great!" exclaimed Digger. "Could I use your phone?"

"Sure." Rick handed over the heavy relic of a rotary phone onto the counter to Digger.

"Got a Yellow Pages?"

Rick looked under the back of the counter and produced a dusty phone book. Everything in the office was dusty. The pin-up calendar on the wall was dusty.

Digger flipped through the Yellow Pages. His eyes made a little *aha!* He began dialing.

"You guys like pizza?"

"Sure."

Digger now spoke into the phone's receiver.

"Yes, I'd like to order three? Three pizzas for Rick's VW Repair, on Valley."

"Yeah, we know Rick's," said the voice on the line.

Rick pantomimed an *aw, man. You don't have to do that.*

"What do you want on your pizza?" Digger addressed Rick.

"Aw, anything, man," said Rick. "No pineapple."

Digger completed the order. "I'll pay cash. That's right. Thanks." He hung up the phone and spoke to Rick. "Thanks for squeezing me in."

The pizzas came, and those who weren't up to their elbows in grease joined in on the pizza party. Pieces were saved for those who still had jobs to wrap up.

Now, all Digger had to do was wait. Rick said that it would be a while.

He walked out onto the sidewalk next to the rushing traffic, with its big rigs and pick-up trucks whooshing by. He looked down one direction, then the other. *Einie, meanie, miney, moe.*

Digger chose east and walked in the winter sun, with its sharp shadows, until the auto places and junk yards disappeared. Now, he walked past fortune tellers and a run-down day care facility. He was getting tired of walking, so he sat on a bus bench and banged his palms on his knees.

After a bit, a public transit bus showed up, and its loud air brakes brought it to a stop.

He climbed aboard the bus and paid his fare. One of the advantages of being near-broke is that you always seem to have exact change. He opted for an all-day pass, rather than hassling with the hassle of hassling later. He made his way toward the back of the jerking bus and found an empty seat near the middle.

He had worked up a mild sweat on his street hike, and now the bus's air conditioning was blowing on it, making Digger feel positively icky.

Digger rode for a while, observing the people on the bus, the changing landscape out the window, and the distinct flavor of his own company.

He saw a K-Mart store and pulled the stop cord.

The K-Mart smelled like his childhood, like popcorn and kids. He bought an Icee at the snack bar and wandered. He inquired about restrooms and used one to great relief.

He got back on the bus and rode farther in the same direction.

He was surprised to see major construction going on on one of the freeways.

Digger hopped off the bus, curious as all get out.

He walked from the bus stop toward the orange flags and up the concrete stairs that emptied out onto a vast section of blocked off four-lane freeway, as desolate and abandoned as any could imagine. There were a few orange cones, but nothing else. It was a desert. It was like something from a sci-fi movie, like he was the last man on earth.

Digger decided to walk on it.

At first, Digger stayed close to the shoulder. Then, as his obsolete fear of traffic and of "getting caught" dissolved, he walked down the very center of the freeway. It was a slight incline, one he hadn't really noticed when driving this exact patch of road before.

How different a place looked on foot, not rocketing past it. It wasn't just a homogenous concrete blur. Each square yard was distinct. You could paint a picture of it, and it would have its own character. There was more vegetation than he had ever noticed, bushes and weeds. There was trash...

When Digger crested the top of the freeway segment, he met a striped wooden barricade, where he climbed down another set of stairs.

He walked until he found a payphone. He dialed the number on the "Rick's VW Repair" keychain Rick had given him. It'd be a few more hours, Rick said. Digger kept walking.

Digger encountered a multiplex cinema and studied the posters. Oh, man. Was he in heaven, looking at movie posters. Some of his heroes did them. Richard Amsel, Bob Peak, Mort Drucker, Drew Struzan... Legends.

Digger approached the box office, where a teenager with braces sold him a ticket for *Real Genius*.

He entered the lobby, and his eyes roamed. He had twenty-five minutes to kill. He didn't want anything from the concession stand. Well, maybe something to drink.

He purchased a large Mr. Pibb and took it to an Asteroids video game, where he played until he ran out of quarters. (Three games.) Most of his sweat had evaporated, and he was feeling pretty close to comfortable again.

Digger entered the theatre and sank into his seat and slumped.

The lights dimmed, and the previews started. Previews were almost as good as the movie. Digger dug watching the little nuggets of Hollywood magic. He hated when the trailer gave away too much of the story, especially the ending.

Then, the movie began. It was neat to see a movie in which being smart was cool.

Finally, the movie finished. It was pretty good. Digger checked his watch, then called Rick's.

His car was done. Rick didn't charge him for labor.

Oh, crap, thought Digger on the bus ride back, *I am hemorrhaging money.*

Digger did some quick math in his head. He probably wouldn't make it another two months on what he had left. He had to come up with a bright idea, and it had to be quick.

Chapter 24 - Mix Tape

Now that he'd gotten his VW bus fixed, Digger came home to take care of something.

He had promised a tape to Mook, his famous new, rock star illustrator, fellow music fan, pal, whom he met at the *Paint It Black* workshop. It was to be a Marshall Crenshaw mix-tape, sort of an introductory sampler to the guy's music.

Oh, man. He couldn't wait. First, he had to choose the blank. He thought he'd go with a TDK SA-60. Great sound. Great mids, highs, *and* lows. Sure, the TDK SA-90s gave you half an hour more of music, but the tape was thinner and more likely to stretch and possibly break over time. Yes, the 60 was the way to go.

Second was figuring out which songs to include and in what order. Digger went to his record collection and pulled out his current and first three MC albums. There were songs, pop gems like "Cynical Girl," "Girls," "Hold it" and the B-side to his hit "Someday, Someway," "You're My Favorite Waste of Time."

The trick was to program each side of the tape like an album, not just a bag of random songs. You had to list what sounded like a decent progression, then add up the times of each song, shooting for a solid thirty minutes per side. You kicked off with something strong, but not your show-stopper. That you saved for later.

Digger started scribbling and crossing out candidates, working and reworking the song order.

Ah, yes. That's it. Nope.

He crumpled up the list. No, the best way to get into Marshall was the first two albums. That's what he'd do. Side A would be his self-titled debut album, and Side B would be his second album, Field Day.

Now, the J-card.

Digger removed the cellophane from the blank tape and popped open the transparent case. He removed the cassette, the blank labels, and the J-card. He sank the cassette into the tape deck, set the recording levels, and hit the *record* button.

While the LP was recording, Digger started working on the meticulous lettering that would list the tracks. Then, that which would go on the spine. Using fine-tip pens and markers, he lettered like a monk, faithfully reproducing the red, black, and white logo from the *Field Day* record.

When he was done, Digger took the tape to the kitchen. While he admired his handiwork, Digger took out Mook's card and dialed the number. He got an answering machine.

"Hey, Mook. This is Digger, from the workshop. We talked about music in your car. Anyway, I made your tape and it'll be going out in tomorrow's mail. Talk to you soon." *Beep!*

He was proud of himself for not sticking his foot in his mouth because, boy! Did he come close!

Digger checked his watch. He had just enough time for a shower before Beverly needed rescuing.

Chapter 25 - Nothing Fancy

That night, Digger wore one of Beverly's husband's suits. It was only slightly big on him, giving him a very fashionable, billowy quality. A small combo played Cole Porter. There was wine. There was cheese.

"This suit is unbelievable. I feel like David Bowie."

"It was Peter's." Beverly's mind suddenly and briefly went somewhere else. "I thought you might like this. I didn't feel like coming alone."

"You kidding? Free food and stuffy talk? I'm in."

Beverly got suddenly wistful. She took in, then let out a deep breath.

"Digger, I'm gonna turn you loose. Have fun. Don't get into too much mischief."

With that, Beverly wandered off, not really engaging anyone, just riding the waves and eddies of the room. She picked up and briefly nursed a drink before abandoning it on a windowsill.

Digger felt uneasy. He'd grown some socially, he thought, but he wouldn't want any sort of pop quiz. He navigated the social waters of the Art Scene, but not yet expertly.

Some rich folk, eager to flex their philanthropic aesthete muscles, raised their voices at key moments to ensure that the room heard them.

Once in a while, Beverly and Digger exchanged affectionate little acknowledgements from across the room. A wiggle of the fingers, a silly face.

Digger drifted into a tight circle of chortlers, mid-conversation. He hung back, standing behind the inner circle, just behind Lawrence Melman, late fifties, a hoot owl in a sweater vest.

Tobin, a snooty forty-something-year-old with expensive glasses and hair full of mousse, was doing some serious brown-nosing.

"You should know. You're the authority on Matisse," said Tobin.

"And Manet," boasted Melman. "*Don't* forget Manet."

"What about that theft in Budapest?" said Tobin, changing the subject.

"The stuff that was recovered turned out to be forgeries! The burglars still have the real stuff!"

"Why would they do that?" asked Digger, going out on a limb to jump into the conversation. "Go through the trouble of having or making forgeries? Why not just steal the stuff and be done with it?"

Melman answered without looking at Digger.

"It bought them time. The hunt for the thieves lost much of its steam when the authorities thought they'd recovered the art. The authorities are more concerned with rescuing and recovering the artifact than catching the criminals. True, both in Europe and here in the States." Melman shook his head, enjoying the spotlight.

"Forgery is so stupid. Especially if it's a copy of a well-documented work, like say the Mona Lisa. Too easy to detect the smallest inaccuracy. Not worth it." Melman continued. "Also, with counterfeits, most don't truly understand how to confine themselves to the period. The counterfeiter *thinks* they understand the period they seek to impersonate, but, a decade later, we see how the work has been projected through the colored lens of the time of its creation!"

Digger was riveted. "It's like watching The Sting," Digger interjected. "That's a '70s take on the '30s. The haircuts look like '70s haircuts, trying to pass as Depression haircuts."

"Precisely." Although he spoke to him, snooty Melman kept his back to Digger.

"I became an expert on art forgery by watching Happy Days," Digger quipped.

"You certainly are a sharp fellow for someone so obviously... young."

"Oh, I'll forgive your mistake. I actually have a rare genetic disorder that gives me the appearance of being very young. I assure you that is not the case."

"Really?" asked another guest. "Do they know what causes it?"

"Yes. Lying." This retort caused an eruption of laughter.

Tobin gave Digger his calling card, insisting that he take it.

"You're quite a character. I think I know some people I'd like you to meet. You'd amuse them."

Beverly appeared. "That'll have to wait. If you will excuse us." Beverly stole Digger away and literally cornered him.

"Digger, do you know how to dance?"

"Not the way I think you mean."

"It's easy. Let me show you. Here."

Beverly showed him a simple box step. He picked it up quickly.

She turned to face him, and they danced. There was no real dance floor and nobody else was dancing, but there was music, lovely music.

The two of them just tooled around a corner of the room. Nothing fancy, no complicated turns, but they danced, and it was nice, really nice. They did this for the remainder of their stay.

After the evening's enjoyment, Digger's newly repaired jalopy bus pulled up in front of Beverly's house. Digger hopped out and opened the passenger door for her. Beverly sleepwalked to the door.

Beverly turned to face Digger. She and Digger exchanged air kisses, and she entered the house. The lonely, lonely house.

It remained dark as Digger's car pulled away.

Chapter 26 - Help Wanted

The next day, Digger consulted his bank book and the cigar box he kept under his bed. $1,250. That was not going to last forever. He didn't want another job. Heck, he was having the time of his life, with the drawing workshop four days a week, the night classes, and his new friendships. The thought of signing up only to row for another slave ship was the last thing he wanted to do, but he had expenses. There was gas, food, art supplies, and now, rent.

He'd have to pound the pavement.

Digger went to a convenience store where he bought a donut, a Pennysaver, and two newspapers. He asked about the "HELP WANTED" sign in the window.

The franchise owners were a family. The flabby kids seemed to use it as their own personal snack box. They ran in and snatched snacks off the shelves, whooping and hollering, then ran out again.

The woman was not the friendliest person Digger had ever met. She looked him up and down and told him he would have to take a polygraph test.

"For a Sip n' Snak?" Digger asked. The woman looked as though them were fightin' werds.

"Lotta employee theft. You want the job? You take the polygraph."

She handed him a business card.

"Here. He handles all our business. It'll cost you $60."

"This gets better and better," said Digger.

"Look, you want the—"

"You want the job, it'll cost you $60. I get it. I get it."

*

The polygraph office was in a complex near the public library and the police station.

The card said that they opened at 10:30. Digger's watch said 9:40.

To kill time, Digger sat down on the ground next to the front door and just perused the classifieds.

How fucking ridiculous is this? Digger thought. *Polygraph. Inadmissible in court, by the way.*

At 10:42, a sturdy flour sack of a man showed up and unlocked the door to the office.

Digger got up from sitting on the ground and dusted himself off before following him in.

The man had a cop moustache and seemed to think that anybody who came through that door was just stopping here on their way to jail. He led Digger to a small room and hooked him up to all sorts of electrodes.

"Do I get a last meal?" Digger joked, getting the very response he expected.

"Is that your real name?"

"Nickname."

"An alias. Have you ever done drugs?" asked Flour Sack.

"Yes. Pot in high school," answered Digger.

"Have you ever stolen anything?"

164

"Yes. Shoplifted when I was a kid, maybe eight or nine."

That concluded the test. No, Digger was told, he couldn't know the test results.

"But, I *paid* for them."

After waiting an hour or so, as directed, Digger returned to the Sip n' Snak, expecting a starting date and hourly rate.

No dice.

The woman said, "How dare you even come back here?"

"Because I smoked pot a few times in high school?"

"The polygraph found your answers deceptive."

"Deceptive? How on earth were they deceptive? You mean I never got caught shoplifting as a kid or smoked pot in high school? Ridiculous!" Digger didn't wait to be dismissed.

Even though Digger didn't want to work for people like these, he felt as though he had been found guilty of something, that he was exiled from a place he didn't like anyway. That didn't soothe his bruised ego one bit.

He'd already wasted half the day, and now he was hungry again. La Flor de Mexico was close by.

Digger saw a similar "HELP WANTED" sign in the window at the La Flor burrito stand and asked the cashier on duty to see the manager. Digger's Spanish was decent enough to communicate with the cashier on duty. His name was Ernie. He told Digger to come back at 2 to talk to the owner.

Digger decided to just hang around. Ernie fixed him up with a burrito and an iced tea. Digger ate this at the farthest picnic bench from the burrito stand, an old car hop joint.

When the owner showed up, Digger was shown around the kitchen and walk-in freezer and offered half check and half cash under the table. He'd be working swing shift, 4 p.m. to midnight, five days a week. He would be the night manager.

"But, there's a catch," said Lupe, the boss. "There already is a night manager. I just know she is robbing me blind. Everybody tells me, but I have no proof. The guys who tell me are illegal, so they're afraid to go on the record. But every time she forgets to close out the register and do the night's final totals, we're way short of our averages, and that's on our busiest nights. I'm absolutely positive that she's skimming off the top," she continued.

"None of the cooks like her, and they're a pretty good bunch. I get complaints from customers. She's rude. She wears shorts and tank tops to work. I mean, we're serving food here. That's disgusting. She's supposed to be the manager, for crying out loud."

"Why don't you just fire her?"

"I don't know. Maybe I'm afraid she'll report me."

"Report you?"

"I don't know. Immigration, the IRS. I got some people here ain't got their green cards yet. Your first order of business would be to fire Diana. That's her name."

This all sounded confusing and loopy to Digger, but hey, he needed a job, and the money was sounding pretty good. As far as firing this existing employee went, he would have to check her out in action before making any rash moves.

"She'll be here in under half an hour," said the boss. Digger got a lump in his throat. The boss locked herself in her office.

She finally showed up, late. Diana.

Diana looked at the window where Ernie was taking down the "HELP WANTED" sign.

She looked as though she knew what was up. She finished her cigarette and then entered the stand.

"You must be the new guy."

"Yeah, hi. You can call me Digger."

She hopped up on the countertop, where she sat and began to howl with laughter.

"Digger? That's your name? Well, *Digger*, you can start by taking the trash out back."

"Isn't that where food goes?" asked Digger, indicating her sitting on the counter, knowing damn well he was just picking a fight.

"Listen, Diana." Diana flinched that Digger already knew her name. "I've been hired as the new night manager, and I'm here to tell you... that you're fired. Sorry."

Diana had a furious smirk on her face. She looked crazy. Digger thought she might pull a knife on him.

"Oh yeah, *Digger*." Diana went for the phone on the wall. "We'll just see about that."

Diana punched in some numbers and waited for someone to pick up. Then.

"Baby, it's me. You won't believe me. Lupe, that bitch, hired some little worm to tell me I'm fired. That's right. Uh-huh. See you, baby." She hung up. "That was my boyfriend." Her face was positively beaming. "You're in for it now."

He must have lived close, because it didn't seem like five minutes before a loud car came rumbling with banda music blaring. It screeched to a stop, and a bald pit bull of a man got out, wearing jeans, cowboy boots, and sunglasses.

Digger grabbed the phone and began to dial the cops until this undershirt full of muscles hung up the phone.

"Hey, flaco. You know who I am? I'm Luis. I'm Diana's boyfriend, and I am your nightmare come true." Luis had a tattoo running up his neck. As Luis' threats escalated, Digger saw behind him the entire kitchen crew, knives out.

"Hey, Luis!" called a large, tall cook. He was missing his front two teeth and looked like a Mexican Jackie Gleason. Luis turned around. The cook continued. "Why don't you just get the fuck out of here and take your *pinche novia* with you?"

The other kitchen pirates shook their knives and made noises of support. Luis was unarmed and clearly outnumbered.

Diana and Luis got into their cars and left, but not without parting glares, glares promising, *I'll be back.*

Digger didn't like the whole vibe. He trembled. He wasn't keen on working a register inside a glass fish bowl, just waiting for some kind of violent retaliation.

He suggested to the owner that she promote Ernie to night manager. Ernie's English wasn't too shabby, and he clearly was a stellar worker.

Lupe, the owner, took the payroll and left in her eggshell Cadillac.

Digger thought it best to just get the hell out of there, pronto.

168

He drove his car a couple of miles from the burrito stand and parked on the street in front of a row of shops, where he spent the next hour circling ads in the paper until he finally just quit.

It was no use. Digger just did not want to work. He wasn't lazy. He was a hard worker. He just didn't want his energy misapplied. He had work, real work, and lots of it, ahead of him. He just couldn't sacrifice what he had going on, not anymore.

Ultimately, Digger decided to just coast until the money ran out. The money he had might last him another couple of months, if he were extra frugal. By then, he might have figured something out.

He saw a street clock. He had better get ready. He had made evening plans with Beverly.

Chapter 27 - We're Not All Cut Out to Be Mothers

That night, Beverly and Digger had a study date. They worked head-to-head on her dining room table on their respective projects. Her drawings were schematics of sculptures to be constructed—lyrical, organic shapes reminiscent of complex lava lamp blobs.

He worked in his sketchbook, brainstorming some ideas he had for his illustration class.

"That's one of the things I like about you, Digger."

"Pardon?"

"You're cool with being quiet."

"Yess'm." With that, they both started cracking up.

"Digger, tell me what you think of these."

Digger got up and stretched. He then came around to her side of the table and looked at the plans she had drawn.

"Well, this isn't exactly my area of expertise, but… they look solid."

"Yes, but Digger, do you *like* them?"

"I really don't know. I mean, they please my eye."

Beverly clasped her hands together in glee.

"Oh, Digger. You're one of the only persons whose opinion means anything to me… when it comes to art."

"Aw, shucks."

Dirty dishes marked the aftermath of a student spaghetti cook-in. Beverly wasn't up to dealing with them right now. They wandered into the living room, where they plopped onto the sofa.

"Ooh, it's late," Beverly yawned.

"I'd better go," announced Digger with a yawn of his own.

"No way. You'll wrap yourself around a tree. You're staying here. "

"Okay. You win."

Digger nestled himself into the sofa. Beverly covered him up with a cozy afghan. She sat on the other side of the sofa. It was a quiet moment.

He closed his eyes.

Beverly spoke into the late-night darkness.

"We had a child, Peter, and I. He wanted one so very much. And I would do anything for him. She really was a remarkable child. Bright, beyond beautiful. We did a lot together. Went to the zoo, read books at bedtime, and baked cookies. You can imagine.

"When she was two and a half, we went on vacation in the mountains. Peter loved camping. We went hiking the first morning that we were there. For most of the hike, Peter carried her, riding on his shoulders. Sometimes, she wanted to do her own hiking.

"There was an accident. We all fell and slipped down a rocky embankment toward a cliff. Peter strained to grab onto her. I grabbed onto Peter. I eventually got hold of both of them, but I am only so strong. I could feel them slipping.

"I could only save one, my child or my husband.

"Now, he doesn't forgive me for the choice I made. He's off, probably in a hotel somewhere, a mess, a total, complete mess, hating me with all his might.

"His sabbatical leave is over in a couple of weeks, and I don't know if he's coming back, if only to jettison me out of his life forever."

Beverly took in a deep, shaky breath. She was sleepy.

Digger sat up, now wide-awake.

She continued. "'Til then, it's just some tuition-free classes (I get them as Peter's spouse), a leave of absence from my freelance work, and not looking forward to the rest of my miserable and lonely life.

"Valentine's Day is coming up. Our anniversary. Happy Anniversary!"

Beverly was groggy. Her head wobbled.

Digger walked her upstairs and tucked her into bed.

He looked over framed photos on the nightstand and dresser.

He peeked through the open master closet, checking out Beverly's husband's fine-tailored suits. He noted the name of the tailor on a sewn-in label. It was the same as the one he'd borrowed earlier in the month.

Digger had something in mind… and he'd need fine threads to do it.

Chapter 28 - Camelot!

In the Design Center parking lot, Digger got ready for the afternoon drawing workshop. He opened a can of lentil soup with the can opener he kept in the car and guzzled it. He then fished some clean clothes out of his car and stuffed them into a gym bag.

He showered in the model's locker room with his eyes closed. Words dribbled out of his mouth, nonsense words. It was like having Tourette's Syndrome. Dribble, dribble, dribble. Words of sadness, words of violence, words of death. *Just kill me.*

He had been talking to his mother again.

The hot water pummeled his back. Oh man, nothing like a shower. He could face the world again.

Digger decided not to go to the workshop after all.

*

Attendance at the afternoon drawing workshop was sparse. Beverly poked her head in. Digger's usual horse was empty. Dean recognized her. His was not a look of warmth. Tony noticed this.

"What's his problem with her?" Tony asked Rachel as Beverly backed out of the door.

Beverly strolled the hallway with no real sense of urgency. She had been hoping to dig up her good old friend Digger for some distraction. Working on her remaining art pieces—most of her assigned work was completed—didn't hold any appeal. She could call Patsy, but Beverly really wanted to forget who she herself was for a couple, maybe a few hours, before the fundraiser tonight.

Beverly dragged her fingertips along the cool of the concrete wall.

Maybe it was time for a life of crime, robbing banks, blowing up hot dog stands, jaywalking…

Maybe Neighbor Kitty was free for a little belly scratching.

*

Parking here wasn't any worse than at the junior college, which still meant it could be plenty bad. It was at some sort of recreation center. Digger had never been here before, but there were plenty of signs and foot traffic to follow. Easy enough. Digger just took his quad-folded flyer and blended in with the crowd as it flowed toward the auditorium. It was the night of Bridget's play.

Digger wore a collared shirt and slacks, the same pair he wore for senior picture day in high school. He wore his leather shoes. He was going more for "appropriate" than "stylish." Like many, he had more taste than money, although that wasn't saying much.

He made it into the auditorium and tried to make his way to the wings of the stage, but the crowd was just too packed and rustling. He figured he'd say hi after the show. Maybe that would be better anyway. He had no idea if having friends or family in the audience made it easier or harder to perform. He consulted the ticket he bought at the ticket window. The show started in seven more minutes. Mob seating.

Digger opted for a seat slightly to the right of the stage. He had read that people's heads relaxed in the direction away from their dominant hand. Digger was right-handed, so his head would naturally settle a little to the left. That seemed comfortable.

A respectable-sized musical ensemble began to play the overture as the lights dimmed.

Digger had never seen *Camelot* before, not the movie, not the play. As far as he was concerned, he was here to support a friend, but, *hey, while I'm here, I might as well learn something.*

Buh-buh-bommmm! The ensemble played. Buh-buh-bommmm!

After a while, Digger latched on. He was riveted.

The songs! The songs were great! *C'est Moi!*

When Guinevere launched into *The Lusty Month of May*, a troupe of handmaidens twirled onstage from the wings.

The sets were remarkable, painted beautifully. Decent casting. Great story.

There was Bridget! None of the handmaidens had the identical costume. Digger quickly recognized Bridget's as the one he had designed for her just a couple of weeks or so ago.

He could hear her voice clearly when she reached the lip of the stage. Otherwise, she blended in nicely with the others. They danced and they whirled and they belted.

At the end, Digger beamed as he banged his hands together in applause, so hard they began to hurt. "Brava!" he shouted again.

After the show, the cast came out for the curtain call. Bridget nearly fell out of her laced-up dress when it came her turn to bow.

When the lights came up, Digger felt like a stooge for not having brought her flowers. He figured he'd ignore that feeling and just make his way backstage. He banged his souvenir program against his leg absently.

"You made it!" Bridget's cheeks were flushed and slick with sweat as she bear hugged him.

"I just wanted to say hi. You were fantastic! Everybody was fantastic!"

"You came! You really came!"

"Thanks for inviting me. Look, I know you probably have a cast party or something to get to. I just wanted to say hi—"

"No! No! Don't go. There are people I want you to meet." Bridget began to catch her breath. Man, did she look yummy in that dress, Digger thought, with her sweaty hair plastered to the side of her head.

"Come on. I'll ride with you, Digger. My car's at home. Let's get out of here."

Bridget navigated while Digger drove. She had changed out of her costume and into a t-shirt and jeans.

The party was held at somebody's two-story house. There were Igloos full of beer and soda. People were hanging on the banisters, sitting on the stairs, lounging in each other's laps, and standing as relaxed as anyone can be doing that.

Conversations and congratulations abounded. Scene re-enactments erupted spontaneously. Digger liked Bridget's friends. He even recognized a few from her birthday party a little while back.

Somebody put on a record, and some dancing broke out. It was Gerry Rafferty's *Right Down the Line*. Bridget turned to Digger.

"Oh, please! Please, please, please!"

Digger got a grin on his face, and he took her hand and led her into the living room, where they danced in place, each holding one hand of the other. They danced for a long time.

After a long and lovely night, Digger dropped Bridget off at her folks' house with a big hug.

"You were great, just great. Thanks for inviting me."

"Thanks for coming." She ran her fingers through his bangs. "Give me a call. I'll cut your hair."

*

Still sweaty from dancing, Digger greeted Kevin with a nod and scooted into the Carrows booth opposite him. Kevin steeled himself.

"Hey, man. I've got some news. I'm going into the Army," Kevin blurted before Digger had a chance to speak.

"The ARMY?!" yelled Digger, startling some of the other late-night Carrows patrons. This news hit him like a shovel to the back of the head. He choked on the words.

"What the hell are you talking about? You're a pacifist. We've been anti-Army since we knew that was a thing. You're no killer," continued Digger.

"Look, man. We're not only the smartest guys in this lame ass town, we're smarter than most of the guys they'll ever meet. Shit, Digger! You speak German! You speak better German than I do!"

"So what?"

"So what is, you didn't *take* German! You picked it up from watching movies and helping me study German!" Kevin was agitated. "Everyone our age is going off to a *real* college or gonna be stuck *here*. I've got shit for grades and a college fund that could buy me a tank of gas. You and I don't have shit here. At least as a mercenary, they'll pay for my school, and I'll get out of this shit hole town."

The two stared at each other as Karen dropped a menu in front of Digger.

After she walked away, Digger stood to leave.

"I can't believe this. You're joining the fucking Army."

"Not joining. Joined."

Digger left the diner and headed for his VW bus. The cold wind slapped his face.

As he cranked the engine to life, he caught sight of himself in the rearview mirror. He looked pale and exhausted. His mouth began to curl, and his brow buckled. His face grew more and more pained.

Kevin was his best friend in the world. They had survived the tedium of Cub Scouts together, prowled the streets and railroad tracks by moonlight, and broken into the high school band room through the small window on the roof.

Digger slammed his forehead against the steering wheel twice. He then slumped, sobbing.

He felt himself drifting farther and farther away from any feeling of security. Something was happening, and it was happening too fast.

After Digger caught his breath, he clicked his turn signal on and backed out of the parking space, then out of the parking lot and onto the road ahead.

He thought he knew Kevin. He didn't know Kevin.

The people who knew Digger didn't know Digger. He would soon demonstrate this.

Chapter 29 - It's *Prowst*

It was a Design Center fundraiser. White wine. Live jazz.

Beverly was transfixed by a large but fragile-looking mobile of orange gossamer glass. She swayed just a bit, lulled by its slowly rotating beauty, until rudely shaken by the unnerving voice of Dini Topp. Beverly couldn't help but overhear, if not eavesdrop.

"These young artists must be made sure that they are on the *right side* of these issues. Like I always say in my classes—"

It was a full-court press as Dini Topp held hostage a trio of the local culturati.

A closer inspection revealed that Rick Jensen, Chairman of Humanities at the Design Center, was also caught in Dini Topp's tractor beam. Beverly couldn't stay away.

"Class-es?" began Beverly, "I thought you taught only one." *One unfortunate class*, thought Beverly.

"More are to follow, Bev. Much more. I have big plans for Design Center."

Beverly *hated* it when people shortened her name.

"The whole direction of Design Center," continued Dini Topp, "must be aligned and fortified by the support of the corporate community."

Dini Topp knew Beverly, the faculty wife. Dini Topp knew *everybody,* and *everybody* knew Dini Topp.

"Rick? Help?" Beverly pleaded.

"Dini does seem to know her stuff, Beverly. She does have her liaisons."

"Lesions?" asked Beverly.

"Liaisons," corrected Dini Topp.

"Easy mistake."

Liaisons with every penis that'll risk the clap, thought Beverly.

"Rick. Please. You gotta help me out here. Are you just going to stand here and let this, *this* talk about making certain that the students think the right things? What about discourse? Independent thought? Free bloody speech? She's talking about making them little corporate mouthpieces." Beverly had truly hoped that Rick would come to her defense, as they were of like mind. "It's no use. Oh, god. Forget it."

Beverly left in disgust as Dean returned bearing drinks for himself and Dini Topp. He was acutely aware that he had missed something.

"Did I miss something?"

Later that night, things had quieted a bit. Beverly caught up with Jensen. She tried a more diplomatic tone.

"You know, Richard. We've got all those young students reading this Modernist and Post-modernist stuff, citing tertiary sources on Freud. Why not have a class on the actual text? Make 'em actually read Freud, for Christ sake."

"Not a bad idea. You know, we already have Gary Minekawa from UCLA. He teaches a strong course on Freud there. I'm sure we could get him to do it for us."

"Freud? shrieked Dini Topp. "Freud was a misogynist! Most of what he's asserted has been disproven. He hasn't done one positive thing for the world."

Beverly was ready to come to blows.

"Freud gave us the first linguistic model of the psyche," said Beverly, inflamed. "What he's asserted has *not* been disproven. It's been improved upon."

"You are so ... unevolved, Beverly. Just a frustrated professor's housewife."

"*I* have a degree from Duke, with a double major in Art History and French Literature, you jackass," Beverly said, seething. "*I* have authored and published a volume on Proust. *I* didn't get here by sucking off every straight man I could scrounge in a New York loft."

"Proust?" asked Richard. He had no idea of Beverly's credentials.

"Some French guy," chimed Dini Topp, misconstruing Richard's inquiry.

"And it's PROWST."

Chapter 30 - Bobby

Nighttime. Malibu. Money.

Digger's bread-shaped jalopy wound through the tree-lined private road that led to the large gate, which led to the multi-level house that could fill the pages of any architecture magazine.

Tobin greeted Digger and led him inside.

They descended the steep stairs into the cool earth. The house's floors did not go up, but down into the Malibu hillside.

"He's just been dying to have you over since I told him about meeting you at the soiree last month."

"You say he's agoraphobic?"

"I don't know that I'd call him agoraphobic, necessarily. He just prefers to ... entertain *here*. You'll be generously compensated, I assure you," said Tobin, really trying to sell it, whatever "it" was.

"You're gonna love this guy. Everybody does."

They emerged into a large cave-type room containing a pool table, three enormous projection TVs, and a saltwater aquarium. There was a large and fully stocked wet bar, a popcorn machine, and thousands, literally thousands of LP records. Every spare inch of the remaining walls was cluttered with everything from original oil paintings to matchbooks to lighted beer bar signs to album covers bearing scrawled sentiments like "RIGHT ON!!" and "ROCK AND ROLL, ALL THE WAY!!" It was high-dollar clutter.

Wearing only boxer shorts and an open, monogrammed bathrobe, Bobby, a wacky hermit-type of indeterminate age, was currently singing to a Fleetwood Mac record blaring on the stereo through a handheld microphone into a PA system.

On the TV screens, Digger saw *The Little Rascals, The Thomas Crown Affair*, a French subtitled film, and an Iranian variety show, all muted.

In his other hand, Bobby held an oversized brandy snifter, sloshing with amber liquid.

Alerted to the presence of guests, Bobby returned the mic to its stand and turned the main volume on the PA all the way down, with a cackle.

"This ... is Digger, the young man I told you about."

"I salute the artist!" And Bobby literally did. He then collapsed into a full-body cackle.

"A drink! A drink for the artist!"

Tobin busied himself with fetching a beverage for Digger.

"So, you're into Art. Right on. Me too. Art's cool. Just got into it. (shakes his head) Man, fucking Andy Warhol." Bobby paused, then broke into a cackle, clapping his hands together.

Tobin brought Digger a HUGE iced tea on a tray, then excused himself from the room.

Bobby took a seat in a huge overstuffed chair, inviting Digger to join him in an identical chair.

"Ain't these chairs great?" Bobby asked. "I just started collecting art. Man, has it opened my eyes. Check this out." Bobby stood and gestured that Digger follow him.

Digger followed Bobby down a long, dark corridor to a large, quite nice, abstract painting hanging on the wall with its own picture light. They still held their absurdly large drinks.

"That there is an original. I'm really not supposed to have it. Supposedly, it's stolen." Bobby shrugged. "But, hey. I want what I want, right?" With that, Bobby turned very serious. Apparently, what Bobby wants, Bobby gets.

They walked past a Nagel poster, into another room. It had acoustic foam on the walls and was full of musical instruments: guitars, a grand piano, a drum set, assorted horns, and string instruments. Also, a life-sized cardboard stand-up of Elvira advertising Coors Light.

Digger sat at the drums. Bobby picked up an electric guitar and strapped it on.

"Boy. You guys." Digger was winging it. He had absolutely no idea what he was saying.

"What do you mean, you guys? You mean art collectors?"

"Yeah. You wacky high rollers." Digger shook his head as if he were in an improv class.

Bobby liked the sound of this. He turned on a guitar amplifier that loudly popped and cracked awake.

"You remind me of these Italian guys," said Digger, "Serious guys."

"Italian guys, huh?"

"Oh yeah. Rich guys. They collect some serious art, rare stuff. Oh, boy."

"Rare stuff? Rare?"

"Oh yeah."

"I gotta meet these guys, Digger! I just gotta!"

"Bobby, I don't think these guys meet with anybody. I mean, I only met their nephew as a fluke."

"I just gotta meet these guys!"

"I dunno —"

"Just get me a phone number! I'll give you ten thousand dollars for a phone number!"

Digger tried not to swallow too hard at the mention of ten thousand dollars.

"Bobby. These are serious cats. They do not just hang out and chat. They do business."

"You're killin' me! Please! I beg you! I'll be your very best friend! I promise! I'll be your very best friend! I know people! I can help you out! Please! I gotta have it!"

Digger clacked the drumsticks together in a 1, 2, 3 count-off.

"I'll see what I can do. No promises, though," Digger said.

They jammed. Digger loved the drums, just loved 'em. He played them in high school and not much since.

Hours later, Digger left with a wave. Bobby leaned against the doorsill with his epic brandy snifter and a cackle.

Digger drove away as the sun rose. His clothes were stiff and salty with dried sweat. He chuckled to himself. It *had* been an adventure, but Digger had no intention of ever seeing this guy again.

But then he wasn't dead yet.

Chapter 31 - Post-Modern Art History

In the low light, students were scattered into small clumps and sparse patches in the Design Center auditorium. Digger was there. Tony, Jonny, and Rachel were also there. Post-Modern Art History.

Some struggled to take notes, others to take naps. The full-timers had grueling schedules, which meant not much in the way of sleep. Dini Topp lectured with a slide show.

Only paying half attention, Tony spoke to Rachel in whispers.

"So, Pashone's looking at my painting and says, get this, *It's like a Monet, but without the thought!*"

Rachel high-fived Tony.

Students' faces ranged from bored to bewildered.

Dini Topp was nothing if not passionate. She was discussing a famous case in which an artist sued a large corporate building for removing a large piece of sculpture that they had commissioned.

"But, it was theirs, wasn't it?" asked a timid student in a Koala Blue sweatshirt.

"It doesn't matter that they commissioned it, that they *paid* for it. You can't just let them roll in and do that! It's like Kent State with these guys! We have to stand up to these, these.. fascists and make it clear to them!"

Digger shook his head, tapping his ball-point pen on his sketch pad impatiently.

"Nobody *owns* a piece of art. The art belongs to the artist and the world. Money doesn't imply ownership. It mandates guardianship. It's Kent State, all over again. Totally."

"Ms. Topp? asked Rachel, her hand raised.

"Dini."

"Ms. Dini. I'm totally lost. You keep saying, Kent State, Kent State. It's Kent State this and Kent State that. What are you talking about? What do you mean? What is Kent State?"

"Just listen to that Crosby, Stills, Nash and Young song, *Ten soldiers and Nixon's coming...*" Dini Topp sang. "That will tell you all you need to know."

Digger had had enough. He spoke without raising his hand.

"Excuse me? You didn't answer her question."

"Yes, I did. You just don't like my answer."

"This is a *required* class in an accredited school," demanded Digger, surprising himself just a little. "Students graduating from here are going to be held accountable to *know* this stuff."

Something in Digger snapped. He no longer gave a fuck about consequences or playing nice. He no longer tried to "meet in the middle."

"You're not the first person to disagree with me," boasted Dini Topp. "I've always been something of a maverick."

"Maverick? How is being inarticulate and ignorant being something of a Maverick?" Digger nearly shouted. "I don't simply 'disagree' with you. I am asserting that one who answers legitimate questions with responses like that is not qualified to teach. Anywhere."

"Holy shit!" squeaked Tony, elbowing Jonny awake.

There was a weak smattering of applause in the back of the room.

"Wha, WHA?" yawned Jonny.

Beverly came in late, carrying two cups of coffee, and sat next to Digger, handing him one. She was auditing the class.

"What'd I miss?" asked Jonny.

Dini Topp now saw them together, Beverly and Digger. Ahhh. Beverly must have found a little chew toy herself. So, they were a united front, one enemy unit, huh?

Bad move, kids. Bad move.

Chapter 32 - Digger, We Can't Do This Anymore

Digger's pockets were full of change when he called from a pay phone in the packed Design Center student lot. He was waiting for the exodus of night students' cars to stop clogging the exits. He dialed home.

"Audrey. It's me."

"No shit."

"Just calling to see if anybody called for me."

There was a long silence. Was that an, I'm checking? Or was that an, Of course not, dumbass? Digger guessed the latter.

"Hey. I was thinking about mom's birthday."

"When are you ever gonna fucking learn?" snapped Audrey.

"What? What is your problem?"

"Not my problem. Your problem. I don't have a problem, Digger. You have a problem. Your mother hates men."

Digger was subtly, but visibly, stunned.

"You've seen the way she treated all those guys she dated. She. Hates. Men. She hates you. You do handstands to please her, and she gives you a fat lip, for crying out loud."

Digger's silence irritated Audrey.

"Come on. You clueless, naive, sap. Mom's right about one thing. You may be Teacher's Pet, but don't know shit about what's been going around you. Ever since we were small, you've worshipped a woman who wishes you were dead. She's always saying you'll amount to nothing."

"She does not." Digger began to kick the bottom of the phone booth with his toe.

"Not to your face. She says that the world will chew you up and spit you out. You have no killer instinct."

A century of silence passed.

"Digger, you can do all the seminars she wants you to, give all the footrubs and make all the fucking Mother's Day drawings you want, Digger. It will never, ever matter. She's always letting you know how you are nothing, that you'll never make it without her, that the world will eat you alive, and that if, by any chance, you make it, you'll have her to thank." More silence.

"So. Anybody call for me?" Digger repeated.

"Some chick."

*

Overlooking the lights of town, Digger and Bridget lay in his benchless VW Bus with the back popped open. Bridget's legs stuck straight out as Digger kneaded the soles of her feet with his thumbs. She let out a groan that usually doesn't come from a clothed woman. This was and wasn't just like rubbing his mother's feet.

"Good GOD," said Bridget with heavy breath. "I'm gonna come right now."

"Bottom of the feet. Lots of nerve endings."

Bridget let out a heavy, erotic sigh and Digger put her foot down gently.

"I have something to tell you. We gotta stop doing this. There's this guy I really like in the theatre group, and we're gonna give it a shot. Thanks for the awesome foot rub. I'll suck you off right now, if you like."

"That's okay. I'm good."

They took in the cold night sky. Digger leaned back and then lay next to her on his stomach, looking out at the twinkle of the town below. His mind was elsewhere.

"Some are free to take their sharp sticks and poke poke poke, while I'm stuck in the cage, constantly being told to just take it. Be yourself, they say. Easy to say if you're like everybody else. So many assholes. I wonder, do I act boldly and honor my natural reactions to their horrible misdeeds or just let karma take care of things?"

Bridget still lay on her back, staring up at the stars that were more visible from the hills.

"I don't know exactly what you're talking about here, Tiger. But remember. You are a part of the Big Everything, Digger. Sometimes, *you* are someone's karma."

She looked at the sky.

"I hope he pulls my hair. I like it when you pull my hair."

Chapter 33 - A Real Meal

As the afternoon drawing workshop concluded and its participants dispersed, Beverly turned to Digger and said, "I'm hungry. How 'bout you?"

"I was gonna grab a couple of microwave burritos."

"Digger!" Beverly scolded. "Those things are garbage, nothing but lard and chemicals. Let me take you to dinner."

The restaurant was located in downtown Pasadena. French. Digger felt underdressed because he was.

"Wow. I've never been to a place *this* nice."

"About time you had," Beverly smiled.

Seated at the table, Digger wasn't clear on how much of the bread he should eat. The waiter came to take their order.

"I'll have the grilled salmon... with the fresh asparagus," ordered Beverly.

"Asparagus? You've got to be kidding."

"You don't like asparagus."

"No way. My mom can eat that stuff by the can. And with gobs of mayonnaise."

"By the can? No, no, no," insisted Beverly. "You've never had fresh asparagus?"

"Can't say that I have," said Digger, just oozing enthusiasm.

"Well, you are in for a surprise."

"With a mother like mine," Digger began, "I'm not too keen on surprises."

This was a whole new world for Digger. One that would surely find him out and eject him. He was learning so much. *At least*, he thought, *I can take this with me, once they bounce me out of High Society.*

Beverly ordered a bottle of red wine and poured Digger half a glass. Digger sat straight up, as if concerned about his young age.

"Don't worry, honey. At these prices, they're not about to start carding you."

Digger brought up the Spain study abroad program offered.

"Oh, you gotta go, Digger. Got to. Every person should travel. Travel is education," she said, sipping her wine. "Every person should have a passport, a good doctor and lawyer, and a place to stash cash, an offshore account."

"Why all of this?"

"Because, Digger," Beverly winked. "Ya never know."

"Ya never know," he repeated. "A friend of mine said that without cash, we're all slaves."

"She's right."

"Well, I am sick and tired of being a slave."

"Look at you, Digger. I'm impressed."

Their food came, her salmon and his steak with pommes frites. The efficient, aproned waiter whisked away.

"Okay, Digger here. Try this."

Beverly fed a reluctant Digger a single stalk of sautéed fresh asparagus.

He chewed the buttery vegetable.

"Hmmm. This isn't all mushy, like the canned stuff. Not bad. Not bad at all. I like it."

"Digger, there may be hope for you yet," said a smiling Beverly.

"God, I sincerely hope so."

Chapter 34 - Threads

The next day, at the figure workshop, there was an exceptional turnout. The place was packed. Tony, Rachel, and Jonny sat on their wooden benches like surfers, chatting between poses.

"They must all be here for Roy Lichtenstein's lecture in the auditorium," Rachel observed.

"You goin', Digger man?" asked Tony.

"I dunno. I'm pretty busy." Digger didn't want to let on that he had no idea who this *Lichtenstein* was. "I've got this assignment and stuff."

"Come on, man! The guy is a legend! The '60s! Pop Art!" Jonny said, taking out a kneaded eraser and stretching it repeatedly. "He did those paintings that looked like huge comic book panels!"

"Can nighttime students come?" Digger asked.

"Who's gonna know? Come on, Digger! They just sold one of his pieces in New York for half a mil! Half a mil, Digger! Oh, man!" Tony clutched his belly in laughter.

"Half a million dollars? You have got to be kidding me," said an astonished Digger.

"Not at all, dude. Not that long ago, a self-portrait of Picasso's—"

"Yo Picasso," Rachel assisted.

"Yeah, Yo Picasso. It sold for, get this, 5.6 million dollars," said Tony with an infectious chuckle.

"Yup! Art goes for big bucks to big schmucks!" said Jonny. They all three laughed heartily at this ridiculous notion. All but Digger, that was.

"You know what, folks," said Digger, suddenly bright-eyed. I just can't. Not today. Sorry."

Digger quickly gathered his gear.

"You're missin' out, Digger! Missin' out!"

He disappeared into the crowd and was gone.

Digger got in his bus and headed for the junior college library. He didn't want to be seen at the Design Center library for some reason that even he couldn't put his finger on.

The hike from the south parking lot was a nice, chilly one, with the strong but gentle winter wind blowing crossways. It was dark, although it was still early. He lugged his canvas shoulder bag, surely making a question mark of his spine.

Entering the library, he slapped his back pocket, locating his wallet in case anybody wanted to see his student ID. They never did. He sipped chilled water at the fountain, then looked for some free table space to set up camp. He set down his bag on a dark wood table and removed his jacket, placing it on the chair.

Digger slowly made his way down the aisle of the Dewey Decimal 700s. Art books. He took down a few, cracked them open, and noted their checkout histories.

The Impressionists. The Mannerists. Rococo (which was Italian for *too much*). These words were emblazoned along the spines of these colossal picture tomes. The propaganda genius of The Sistine Chapel, with its heaven-sprawling angels, and the propaganda genius of J.C. Leyendecker, the American Leni Riefenstahl, with his handsome ceramic gods, all canonized and gathering dust as these books were checked out less and less frequently.

Digger took a formidable stack of reference books back to his library campsite. He arranged the stacks in an order that made sense to him. There was a book containing the writings of Michelangelo, huge picture books on Picasso and Matisse, and some slim volumes on Modigliani and Chagall, produced by budget publishers.

Drawing. Lines, tones on paper, or perhaps a cave wall. Such an abstract area for abstract thinking. Meaning, in the most narrative sense, is completely optional, and, for Digger, rather pointless. No, to him, drawing was all about tension, push, and pull. It was about the light source, the core shadow, and the turning edge. It wasn't about feelings, about weeping, or about political slogans.

Digger did not linger over the masterworks before him. No, he hunted. He sniffed and stalked. He scoured the images. He was looking for something, something elusive but specific. He looked for it in the sparse cartoonishness of Chagall. No, not there. He looked for it in the elongated necks of Modigliani. No. No dice. Wait a minute. Matisse.

Digger had found it. Matisse.

Another idea hit Digger. He fished around in his shoulder bag. Aha! There they were, like a school of slippery fish, the student credit card application/brochures. There must have been seven of them, all from different banks. He didn't want to wait for the mail service. Too slow. Perhaps if he visited local branches, maybe that could speed things up a bit. He'd go first thing in the morning.

Digger's car pulled up to the guard station that was lit up like a fish tank. Levi was browsing a true crime magazine. He got up from sitting atop his high stool to greet Digger. Levi was built like a refrigerator and projected an air of calm that was not the same as harmlessness.

"Hey Levi, how would you like a suit?" Digger couldn't help but grin from ear to ear. "How would you like a *really nice* suit?"

A few days later, a large hand-lettered paper sign in the window of Beck's Art Supply read, "Everything Must Go. Grand Closing."

Oh, no, Digger thought. He felt an ache in his heart.

He entered the store. The proprietor acted the same as usual. No difference. He seemed unaffected by the fact that he was going under.

Digger stocked up on old crap, bottles of arcane ink, ancient boxes of conté, pastels…

"I give you good price," said the jovial proprietor. "Closing up the store for good. I give you good price."

Digger kneeled in the corner of a room adjacent to the main room. He was surrounded by stacks, towers, and landslides of antique books.

He mined these, searching only for the largest, books of maps, portfolios of faded prints, etc. Digger picked one up and looked at its blank endpapers. Their yellowed age was obvious, but they were not overly brittle. Digger flipped to the publication date. 1929. This would do just fine.

Atop one of the ragged piles, Digger found a plastic case labelled "Easy Italian." It contained an eight-cassette

Italian language course. One of the cassettes was missing, but the booklet was still there.

Digger made several trips to the checkout counter, much to the delight of the proprietor.

"You," said the proprietor, ringing up Digger, "You gonna make great art with these things!"

"Yessir," answered a grinning Digger, producing one of his brand-new student credit cards.

Digger had gotten the name for this tailor shop from the label inside Beverly's husband's suit. He politely declined a complimentary coffee drink from the tailor's assistant as he sat in a highback chair. Levi stood in front of a three-way mirror, on top of a small alterations pedestal, while the tailor took his measurements with a tape measure and chalk.

"Young man, are you sure you can pay for all this?"

"Levi, that's my department. You just worry about your part." Digger pounded his palms against his knees.

"No matter what I say to you," instructed Digger, "you don't respond in any way."

"Gotcha. I gotta tell you. I'm glad I'm not the only one who's nervous."

"Nervous. Excited. Tomato. Tomahto," quipped Digger.

"Man, nobody says tomahto."

"You don't speak any Italian, by any chance. Do you?"

Levi looked at Digger without dignifying the stupid question.

Digger paid the rather hefty bill with a shiny new student credit card.

The Pasadena Post Office was one of the most beautiful things eyes could ever lay upon. It was grand, a mini-museum, a little Louvre, with its stained glass and turn-of-the-century post office boxes.

Digger made it to the passport window. They weren't open yet. He took the opportunity to close his eyes for a moment and rest. He never really needed much sleep to function, but lately he'd been running on fumes. He felt hollow, like a scraped-out gourd.

The passport window opened, jarring Digger and making him flinch.

"Excuse me. I received my passport and the name…"

"Is it wrong?" asked the clerk.

Digger thought long and hard about what it could mean to have a passport with the wrong name on it.

"You know. Come to think of it. Never mind. My mistake."

At a pay phone outside the post office, Digger took out Mook's card and force-fed the slot a handful of quarters. New York. Long distance.

The phone rang. A machine picked up, *again*. Digger left another message. He was starting to feel like a nuisance and a chump.

Digger then looked up a travel agent in the Yellow Pages. He took out a fan of credit cards that he'd gotten from the vultures at Design Center's Spirit Week and plucked one out.

"Yes. I would like to purchase three round-trip tickets to Chicago. Thank you. Yes, I'll hold."

Digger held his breath nervously. Why should he be nervous? There was nothing illegal about a young man buying airline tickets and making hotel reservations to break in his own, recently granted, credit card, was there?

"You're back? Great. I would also like to book two suites, please. No. On different floors, please."

"I'll need a credit card number to complete the booking," the agent said.

"Yes. Thank you," Digger said. "Here's the number."

That went well, he thought. *But would the rest?*

Chapter 35 - Feel the Bone! Draw the Flesh, but Feel the Bone!

Digger steadied himself before entering the afternoon figure drawing workshop. He felt naked, as if everybody knew exactly what he was up to. When he entered, he swam in the fumes of fear, fear of exactly what?

He wasn't exactly sure. He had yet to do anything wrong. He was just a young student, here to draw the figure in whatever style he saw fit. Many copied master drawings or made studies in their styles. Nothing strange about that.

Amidst all those sweating out their figure work, Digger—after a few warm-up sketches—began his master drawings, using the charcoal, old bottles of ink, and the brittle endpapers from the huge dollar books. It didn't take long for Digger's nervousness to dissipate and for his focus to return.

The model was a Puckian man in his early thirties with curly hair and a dancer's body. He folded himself like a Swiss Army knife and held it, all the time with a small and practiced smile frozen upon his lips.

Digger stared a long time at the model, until finally unleashing his charcoal like a sabre. He lay in curve after countercurve until he felt that one more line would destroy it. Dean passed behind Digger and made a face that indicated some mild confusion. He kept moving.

Taking a break while the model's pose continued, Digger stretched his legs, perusing the drawings-in-progress around the room.

He stopped at Dean's. It was time to bury the hatchet. He lightly punched Dean's shoulder.

"Looking solid, man. Good job, Dean."

Dean nodded an uneasy thanks before he could stop himself.

Digger continued his rounds until stopping at Pashone, who laid down his charcoal pencil and left his easel to stroll with Digger.

They neared Digger's horse. Digger had covered his drawing with a blank piece of paper.

"Come on," began Pashone. "Let's see what you're hiding."

Digger's heart rate went up. Digger revealed the drawing, its curves and countercurves, its chamois lay-in. Pashone looked at the drawing. He leaned forward to touch the paper, but stopped himself.

"Matisse. You're doing Matisse," Pashone said in what could approximate approval.

"What class is this for?"

Dean just glared at them, jealous of Pashone's attention.

That's it. He'd had it.

He knocked over his own horse, sending his drawing pad and tools crashing and scattering across the floor, startling the entire room, before storming out.

The room fell silent. Then, unexpectedly, it exploded with scattered laughter. Even Pashone's eyebrows jumped. His attention returned to Digger's drawing.

"Yes. I see it. The flattening of the figure. Those curves." Pashone paused. "Very nice."

After a bit, Digger left for the men's room. He entered as Dean was leaving. They bumped shoulders.

"Watch where the fuck you're going!" yelled Dean.

Dean shoved Digger hard, sending Digger crashing against the stall door. Digger quickly regained his balance and met Dean's stance in alpha-male, antler-locking mode. It was a jumpy moment. The gunfighters stood eye to eye. Digger trembled.

Digger scoured Dean's face, searching, searching, until ... he finally saw it.

Digger smiled. It was like looking in a mirror. He saw Dean's guilty conscience. Digger was not afraid of this guy.

"Ah. There it is. It must have always been there." Digger's unblinking stare was starting to freak Dean out.

"I see the flaw in the design. It's like looking in a mirror."

Gunfighter stare down. Dean blinked first. Digger smiled.

Dean had a guilty conscience but no real killer instinct. That's why his work always looked so unfinished. No killer instinct. Digger knew something about that. But all of that had just changed for Digger.

Digger returned to Room 109 just as the model took the podium. They said Pashone had left for the day.

Digger picked up his horse and lifted it high above his head, moving across the room, right next to Dean's, uncomfortably close, and everybody seemed to notice.

"This will be a twenty," announced the model.

The model struck a pose as Digger made himself comfy in his new spot.

Dean began to lay out his drawing. With tentative strokes, he indicated wobbly egg shapes for the head and rib cage on his pad of white bond paper.

Digger narrated his own efforts in a whisper, for Dean's ears only.

"No, no, no!" said Digger, imitating Pashone. "So many amateurs begin with their indecisive little egg shapes! No authority, no precision at all!"

Digger's pencil, in a few graceful slashes, laid in very soft and light lines of dynamic gesture. He authoritatively blocked in a set of precise and sharp geometric approximations of the rib cage and hips.

"Bridgman, man! Think Bridgman!"

Dean seemed to tune Digger out.

"Angles! Not slop! Angles!" Digger insisted.

The tip of Dean's pencil swirled, 'round and 'round, darkening his soft little shapes.

"Where's that joint, Dean? How can you even *think* about the sag of the skin, the muscle, the hang of that contour if you *don't know where the joint is*?!"

Digger spun out lines that looked like ribbons, confident, powerful, and beautiful. His left hand rested in a fist against his hip.

"Feel the bone! Draw the flesh, but feel the bone, Dean!"

Dean couldn't help it. His eyes flickered to Digger's pad.

A student moved in to stand behind and between them, watching Digger draw. More followed suit.

"Use your arm, man!" hissed Digger.

Dean swung his arm, trying to do like Digger.

"Your arm!" Digger was no longer whispering.

"I AM!!" Dean was slashing and failing, burning and crashing.

The timer went off, and the model broke the pose. It was like Digger and Dean broke the tape at the end of a race. There were the customary sighs and stretches around the room.

A female student seated at her horse began sharpening her pencils with her X-acto knife.

Dean huffed and puffed with adrenaline. His eyes were wide and without focus. He faced his drawing but saw nothing.

Digger got up and slapped Dean on the upper arm and leaned in, close to Dean's ear. He whispered, once again imitating Pashone.

"Don't worry, kid. Better to find out now than to waste half your life finding out, eh?"

Digger walked away as a few students closed in on his drawing and studied it, some without audible comment.

The female student, sharpening her charcoal pencil with an X-acto knife, slipped and sliced her thumb *clean off*!

Blood geysered and spurted. She clutched the wound, shrieking.

Her friend dashed to the sink and wet a stack of paper towels.

Digger left the room.

He needed some air. He headed down the slick and clean cement hallways toward the double doors that led outside.

He shook off thoughts of Dean. That clown didn't matter, not in the big picture.

His mind's eye stared straight ahead. The thoughts of possibility nearly made him dizzy.

Digger was going from a kid with a knack for drawing to a young man with a *future*. The Design Center was not just a chance to enhance one's chops a hundredfold. It was, if the brochures were to be believed, the beginning of personal and professional connections that would last his entire lifetime.

His eyes ran the length of exposed pipes overhead. They were painted black, turning function into an aesthetic that Digger was falling in love with. No clutter. Sleek. He belonged here. He never wanted to leave.

Dini Topp had a small stack of mail in her hand as she clopped down the hallway. She flagged Digger down at the sight of him, breaking through the fog of his wandering thoughts.

"Hey! Hey, Digger!"

Digger approached her. "Yeah? I mean, yes?"

"Here. Save the school a stamp." She smiled, handing Digger an envelope addressed to him.

Digger began to open it, but stopped.

"Should I open it now or wait 'til I get home?"

"Why wait?" said Dini Topp, still smiling.

Digger tried to keep his face in check, but he was secretly excited. Was this an early grant check? A scholarship formality? A loan installment?

Her smile creeped Digger out. He scanned the letter. His heart sank.

"Says here, no scholarship." Baffled Digger's eyes flared. "But I thought I was a 'shoo-in'."

"Who can say Digger?" said Dini Topp, sounding way too chipper. "It's all who you know, as they say. Go ahead and ask your friend."

"My friend?"

"Your friend Beverly. She can explain things to you, perhaps during my class, while I'm trying to teach?" Dini Topp spoke cheerfully. Her words didn't match up with her doughy face. "I'm sure you'll be seeing her soon. You two are always, you know, around."

The following day, Kevin showed up at Digger's job at the balloon factory around lunchtime, bearing submarine sandwiches and canned sodas. He didn't see Digger's bus parked on the street, so he came up the walkway and pulled the door open.

The blast of cold air conditioning made him realize just how sweaty he was. The pool of young women gave him alley cat thoughts.

"Hi, I'm here to see Digger," Kevin announced to the room in general.

A few of the young women looked at each other to see who would draw the short straw. A woman with stringy brown hair let out a sigh and rose to meet Kevin.

"Let me get the boss." She walked the maze of desks and copy machines, disappearing down a hall. She re-emerged trailing the boss into the room.

"You want Digger? He don't work here no more."

Kevin recoiled from this blow but soon recovered and was tempted to offer a sandwich to one of the lucky ladies.

That night, Kevin pulled a late-nighter at Carrows, alone.

He wore his field jacket indoors but couldn't help but feel a chill, not the chill of winter outside, not the chill of the air conditioning that was always set at the wrong temperature, but the chill of one losing a friend. Would he ever get his friend back?

Chapter 36 - Money, Real Money

Digger showed up at Carrows when he knew Karen was likely to be working. He spotted her yellow Honda Civic in the back of the parking lot.

He grabbed a menu from the hostess' stand and took his usual seat. The hostess came out, chewing some food, and gave Digger the stink eye for not waiting to be seated.

Karen plunked down an iced tea with lemon in front of him, then just stood over him with her hands on her hips.

"I know you like it with no lemon. I just like messin' with you." Karen said, fishing the lemon out with a long spoon. "You just missed your friend by an hour or so."

"My loss."

"Okay, cowboy. I'll leave you to your own devices," Karen said before heading toward the salad station. "Just holler if you need me."

Digger sketched up a storm in his sketchbook. He had out his Grey's Anatomy and was referring to, but not copying from, it.

On paper, Digger flayed the figure, peeling back layer after layer of skin, membrane, and fat to expose the muscles. He would then carefully liberate each one, isolating and then removing them until only bone remained.

He did this all on paper, scratching and scraping his ball-point pen, shading with a shower of thousands of parallel strokes. On paper, Digger was The Spanish Inquisition. Merciless.

Besides all of this, Digger was an exceptional caricaturist, although he came from the political cartoonist's tradition of only caricaturing those he disliked. One of his considerable strengths was to draw people's likenesses from memory. His sketchbook was a virtual yearbook, a who's who of the loud, the rude, and the cumbersome.

They were all wonderful, dementedly whimsical, but he was currently putting the finishing touches on what just might have been his masterpiece, a gruesome and nightmarish, yet unmistakable likeness of Dini Topp. Dini Topp, academic fraud. Dini Topp, saboteur. Dini Topp, mortal enemy.

"Am I in there?" Karen asked, having returned to check on Digger.

"No way."

"No way? I feel insulted."

"Trust me. You don't want to be in here," said Digger, indicating his sketchbook. "I wanted to know when you're free to talk."

"We can talk right now, darlin'."

"No. Not here," said Digger, chipper, yet eerily so. Karen's face read puzzled.

"Where we can talk alone, at length?" he continued.

"Now, what's this all about?"

"Money. Real money."

"Sugar, say no more." Karen turned her head to yell. "Maria! I'm takin' my break!"

They met at Karen's Honda Civic in the parking lot.

"What about your friend? Is he in on this?"

"No. Kevin is busy," Digger half lied.

"Now, what did you have in mind? I do believe I heard the words, 'real money.'"

"For starters, I'm gonna need you to come to Chicago with me. You in?"

Chapter 37 - Drawings, and Other Things in Need of Fixing

For the next few days, Digger was a bit jumpy. From his bedroom, he listened carefully for his mother or Audrey to come home. The wind howled outside. The leaves whirled and crashed against his window.

On his bed, Digger had a large, brand-new black drawing folio, fastened with black string on one side. He untied the string and laid it open, then turned to his makeshift drafting table.

On the table lay twenty-two figure drawings in a stack. Each drawing was in the style of Henri Matisse, made in the afternoon workshop, under the noses of everyone at the Design Center.

He scrutinized the first drawing. He had been careful not to disguise the characteristics of the model. It would make sense that these "lost" sketches were from a single session with a single model–no need to complicate things. With simple contours, he gave the chair the look of chairs he'd seen in Matisse's paintings.

This one passed inspection. It was a go. Digger laid it inside the open folio on his bed. He continued until he had chosen twenty solid drawings. He would destroy the two runner-ups.

Digger's eyes lingered upon the final drawing, the one that now sat atop the others in the folio. Before he covered the drawing with a giant piece of acid-free buffer paper, he told the stylized charcoal figure study, "Pretty good. Pretty damn good."

He needed to "fix" the drawings by applying a layer of resin, skim milk, or mastic, so that they would not smudge. He couldn't use a contemporary aerosol fixative. Any art lab would detect that instantly.

Digger realized he needed space to work uninterrupted. He *could* ask Beverly if he could use her garage. What a stupid idea. Why involve her in this? No. A hotel room. That was the answer.

*

The front desk at the small hotel got Digger's name wrong, and he did not correct them. He asked for a non-smoking room away from the pool. The less traffic and noise, the better.

After checking in, Digger lugged in an overnight bag as well as his book bag and a large black portfolio full of faux Matisse drawings.

He took a shower to wash the day off him and recharge his batteries. Standing in just jeans and a t-shirt, Digger spread out the contents of his book bag–assorted resins and painting oils, inks, and a half-gallon of skim milk. He'd also purchased an old atomizer. You blew into it, and it made a spray of whatever liquid you filled it with. It was not unlike his Paasche airbrush.

Some clothesline, clothespins, and Audrey's hair dryer were also spread out on the bed.

He flipped through one of the ancient books he'd purchased at ancient Beck's Art Supply. It detailed how some of the older artists fixed their drawings. There was dipping the drawings in a gum bath. Digger looked at the bathtub in the hotel bathroom. No, there was no time for the kind of trial and error it would take to come up with reliable results. He'd likely wind up destroying half the drawings during the learning process. No. A thin resin solution blown through an atomizer would be the answer.

Okay. Digger cleared off the bed and then laid his first drawing flat upon it. He blew a light mist of diluted resin above the drawing, not directly at the drawing, letting the microscopic droplets drizzle onto the surface from above, trapping the charcoal dust and adhering it to the paper. He did this in thin layers, drying each layer with the hair dryer, set to the next-to-lowest setting. It took several passes, several layers to satisfy Digger.

He then set up a production line so that he could spray many drawings at a time. He set the thermostat for eighty-nine degrees for maximum drying power. He sprayed the drawings on the bed, then hung them on the clothesline to dry before hitting them with another pass.

Digger hadn't checked the time when he really got going, but he knew that he had checked in at roughly 8 p.m. It was now coming up on 3 a.m. The place was beautiful. Nothing but ink and charcoal drawings, covering the bed and a great deal of the floor.

Drawings hung from the indoor clotheslines that divided the room into slices. He loved this stuff. The smell of the fixatives, the wonderland of sketches. And, if all went according to plan, the money would help him leave the stratum of all the people he had known, the people from his tar pit of a town, his psycho poison family, even Kevin, whom he was starting to feel he had outgrown.

No, Digger was sliding into his truer and truer self. He had to start cutting close ties. He could not risk being observed too closely.

Chapter 38 - A Deadly Decision

Beverly was at Vroman's bookstore on Colorado Blvd., one of her two favorite places on Earth. The other was the library. She just had to get out of the house.

Books, books, books. Books were Beverly's world. How often she adored just sinking into a good book while Peter did his research or graded his papers.

She maneuvered her tiny body around the stacks of best-sellers and staff picks like a helicopter around the Mexican pyramids. She strode along the shelves, running a finger along the spines. Books on Cindy Sherman, books on Man Ray, books on Art Deco, books on poisons. A writer's guide to death and killing. A book on sale.

Beverly flipped through a few of them. A formality, really, as she had already decided to purchase everything she had plucked from the shelves. She called it a day once she had an armload.

At the cash register, an aproned young woman asked Beverly if she had found everything "okay." She had a piece of colorful mesh tied into her hair, a la Madonna.

"Yes, thank you."

The aproned young woman rang Beverly up and closed out her register, ready for her break as Beverly left the store.

Parked at the meter, Beverly started her Volvo, and it made a funny burning smell. She had better get it back to the shop. Normally, Peter would be her ride. Normally. Maybe Patsy would be free.

She patted her cornery sack purchase on the seat next to her and turned on the radio. It was Big Country. Peter had always liked how the Scottish band's guitars sounded like bagpipes.

Not exactly peppy, Beverly was in a better mood than she would have expected. She removed the small, brown bottle from her purse. She just held it in her hand before putting it back.

Hand over hand, she smoothly turned the steering wheel of the Volvo, mouthing along with the radio as she pulled into traffic.

Back home, Beverly poured herself the last of a bottle of red. She closed the book on Cindy Sherman and flipped through the poison book, sitting cozy in her recliner. There had to be enough in the bottle for two doses, she mused, thinking of the small, brown bottle on the end table next to her.

Dini Topp crashed into her mind. Dini Topp. Dini Topp stood for everything Beverly despised. She was not just ignorant, she was dangerously stupid, stupid with influence. She was Beverly's Natural Enemy.

Beverly had come to see her own life as something disposable. There was no drama in this thought. Just a simple fact.

Beverly then smiled broadly.

She was going to kill Dini Topp.

Chapter 39 - The Swindle

The hotel lobby was an Art Deco dream, with its elegant curves and ziggurats.

Clive, a granite handsome man in his early fifties who had never made small talk in his life, entered the grand hotel lobby with his wiry assistant. He was a fixer for the family of Bobby Werner, Recluse Guy.

The two met up with Melman, the pompous art expert from the soireé Digger had attended a month or so ago.

"Can you believe these exquisite chairs?" Melman pronounced the word "exquisite" as if it got stuck in his throat. They walked at a clip more suited to Clive than to Melman.

"God, I hate Chicago," sneered Clive. "Okay, *Sister Wendy*. You just tell me these things are fakes, and we can leave. Then, you can go back to your wobbly wooden podium and banging grad students,"

"Although the likelihood of these being indeed undiscovered Matisse drawings is slim, the prospect is a bit exciting," said a gleeful Melman.

"And, you'd know an authentic Matisse," said Clive with some skepticism if not outright derision.

They reached the elevator. Clive nodded to his assistant, directing him to hit the UP button.

"Oh, don't you worry. If anyone will know, it will be I. And, if I say they're legitimate, they're legitimate. If I told Sotheby's that this handkerchief was a Robert Campin, they would sell this handkerchief for two million dollars. Of course, I would double-check these by having lab tests done. Make sure that the materials were verifiably consistent. A formality. It's my word. My word is law," boasted Melman.

"So, Melman. How much would you have to be paid to say that a kerchief was a Robert Campin?"

They reached the elevator. With a soft *bing*, the doors opened and the three stepped inside. Melman was genuinely insulted.

"There is not enough money in the world to get me to do such a thing. If they are fakes, I keep only my retainer. However, if they happen to be genuine Matisse, I want only one of the drawings as payment, promising never to allow this to go public." Melman touched his index finger to his lips. Clive stabbed the elevator buttons.

"I know your terms." Clive looked to the ceiling. "Jesus, fucking Christ, Bobby. What the hell is it you've gotten yourself into this time?"

"You know, this isn't the first time he's done something like this," offered Melman.

They reached their floor and exited the elevator.

"No foolin'," said Clive, who'd already had enough of this guy.

In a lavish suite, Digger had a semi-circle of display easels arranged.

Slicking his hair back and donning some designer fake glasses, Digger went from Clark Kent to Super Euro-Dandy.

He nervously kept repeating to himself, "Con is short for confidence. Con is short for confidence..."

Digger intercepted Clive, Melman, and Clive's assistant at the elevator door and redirected them.

"*No in quest modo*. No. This way," says Digger in a thick Italian accent.

Digger led them down the lavish hall. Clive's assistant shook his head slightly and gave Clive a look that said that he did not recognize Digger. Clive frowned.

"I recognize you from the faxes," said Digger.

Clive was livid. Digger was obviously too young to be The Guy.

"What the hell is this? Are *you* The Guy?" Clive directed his question at Digger.

"I am Marcello. My uncle is 'The Guy,'" Digger said with a slight bow.

Digger stopped at the door of Suite 1246. He rapped thrice, rapidly.

The door popped open.

Clive was hyped up to take alpha male control of the situation.

The covered easels stood like a firing squad.

An immaculately dressed Levi sat in a plush chair nearby.

"First of all," began no-nonsense Clive.

"You will stand over here, please," gently ordered Digger, trying his best to take control the situation.

"I've brought ..." began Clive, eyeing Levi sideways.

"Mr. Melman. Yes. We know of Mr. Melman," said Digger.

Both Clive and Melman were taken aback with this recognition, although Melman's vanity immediately surfaced. He liked being recognized.

"I," Digger scoured Clive's face, "do not know you."

Digger's unblinking stare bored into Clive's face.

"No," began Digger, still sporting the Italian accent. "You two will leave. Levi?"

Levi merely shifted his weight.

This made Clive and company uneasy.

"Just wait a damn minute," Clive finally said.

"This is not Christie's, and you are not here on your own personal errand. You may go."

"I …" Clive was stymied.

"The man I was to meet would know a Matisse when he saw it. He would not need Lawrence Melman to hold his hand. You may return to your employer now. I'm sure he will be understanding and forgiving about his Matisse."

Clive found himself in deep doo-doo. Bobby Werner, the Recluse, may be a loon, but his family did not take failure or disappointment well.

"Please. Stop." Clive pleaded, changing his tack. "I'm sorry if I have offended you. I assure you, I am new to this and unaccustomed to facilitating such—"

"Gentlemen's agreements?" asked Digger.

"Gentleman's agreements."

Digger stared at Clive for a bit longer, as if waiting for him to melt, until.

"You will follow me, now," commanded Digger.

"But."

Clive gestured questioningly at the easels. Digger flipped over two of the easel cover sheets, revealing a menu for the hotel restaurant and tonight's featured entertainers in the lounge. (One did magic!)

"We go now," Digger ordered. He then pointed at Clive's wiry assistant. "Not you. You stay here." The assistant looked to Clive for an answer, but he never got one.

Digger led Clive and Melman out of the suite. Digger took off at quite a clip.

"Not the elevator," instructed Digger, when they reached it.

Bursting in through the side door, Digger, Clive, and Melman trotted down the service stairs.

Clive's assistant stayed with Levi. Eventually, the assistant tried to make small talk with Levi, but Levi followed orders and was as silent and steadfast as a guard at Buckingham Palace. Levi tried not to be nervous.

Digger paused briefly at a metal door before passing through it.

They came to the door of another suite. 956.

A semi-circle of display easels stood away from the tall windows, curtains drawn. Each drawing bore a cover sheet. Karen stood off to the side, her hair up in a tight beehive. She wore a tailored suit, equally stylish and businesslike. She jotted in a small notepad, never looking up, never saying a word.

Digger, Clive, and Melman entered.

Clive had calmed a little bit, returning to a slight skepticism.

Digger's hand made a sweeping "be my guest" gesture.

One at a time, Melman looked over the drawings. He had a loupe and a poker face. Melman really was no clown.

Clive pulled Melman aside for a private word.

"So, Melman. What do you think?"

"Buy them. Buy them all," Melman hissed.

"We should still have a lab look at them, right? Check out the paper and whatnot?" asked a rather concerned Clive.

"Don't bother. Do it. Do it now before he has a chance to change his mind!"

"Now, just wait just a minute."

"I will not lose out on my Matisse due to your ineptitude!"

"Gentlemen," Digger spoke from across the room, rubbing his hands together as if to warm them. "So. Which of these interest you?"

*

A thin clerk in his thirties returned his phone to its cradle and punched a few keys on his desktop computer in a bank in Switzerland.

The clerk took a small printout from his printer and carried it to a standing desk, where his female superior signed it.

An automatic counting machine fired out a shuffle of large foreign bills.

They were stuffed into large envelopes and taken to a large vault where they were placed in a safe deposit box.

*

Levi, Digger, and Karen sat side by side. Business class. Non-stop.

Levi looked upon his new threads with satisfaction. Karen ordered a Bloody Mary, then returned to her small notepad that contained a half-finished crossword puzzle.

Astonished, Digger spoke directly to the space in front of him, with no trace of an Italian accent.

"They bought 'em all."

Karen and Levi shut their eyes for some rest. They had no questions for Digger. They never asked, *How much are we getting paid?* Or w*hen will we get it?* No, they had asked nothing.

Of course, the one obvious question to be asked was, *Will we be caught?*

Chapter 40 - Tailing Dini Topp

Beverly slid into her Volvo and turned on the radio. Paul McCartney's *No More Lonely Nights* played for her pleasure. She put on sunglasses and leather driving gloves, although neither of them was necessary on this overcast day. Beverly just felt like dressing up, playing the role of what was she? Private eye? Assassin?

She drove to the Design Center and parked in the faculty lot.

Beverly would wait. She was on a stakeout. Luckily, she had hit the Little Girls' Room prior to starting what she thought of as her "shift."

She took in a long breath, then exhaled it like cigarette smoke. She drummed on her steering wheel until she saw her. Dini Topp.

Beverly didn't duck or otherwise try to hide. Nothing looked more conspicuous than somebody trying to hide. Why lie when you can just say nothing?

Dini Topp carried a full load of files, clutched to her bosom, along with a leather attaché case. She balanced a coffee with all of this. It was tucked under her chin atop the stack of papers.

She unloaded her payload into the backseat of her white BMW before getting in and revving up. She blasted

"Sunday in the Park with George" so loud that you could hear it through her rolled-up windows.

Dini Topp backed out of her spot like a crazy person, then shot off toward the parking lot exit. Beverly followed, but not too closely. She let another car get in between them. That's what they did in the movies when they were tailing someone.

At the base of the hill, Dini Topp went straight through the traffic light where Beverly usually turned left. Beverly followed her to a Kinko's, where she waited across the street for Dini Topp to conduct her business.

Beverly was hoping to eventually follow her to her home. She'd never been there, so she had no idea what to expect. Guard dogs? A gate? What exactly was the plan here?

But she knew that the best thing to do was wait, wait for opportunity to present itself. Don't force or try to create a situation. Just be patient. Wait for the opportunity and seize it. *But how long must I wait?*

She followed Dini Topp around town until eventually her gas gauge warned her to stop. There was no law, Beverly thought to herself, against doing something ridiculous and feeling foolish.

Murder, on the other hand…

Chapter 41 - Off the Beaten Path

Digger pulled up to his house and parked his VW bus on the street.

His breathing was still rapid and shallow, having just pulled off the art forgery swindle. Now was not the time to deal with Audrey or Mother.

He just couldn't go in. He couldn't run the risk of being seen like this, all out of sorts and pressed for an explanation. He pulled away from the house.

Digger's car hobbled up the driveway of a cheap motel. He checked in and went to his room.

Wearing only a towel around his waist, Digger sat on the edge of the large, stiff motel bed, fidgeting manically. Much weighed upon him. The con, was it too easy? Was he on the run, or just on Easy St.?

Oh, my god, Digger thought. *I did that. I really did that.*

He turned the motel TV on. He bathed in its flickering glow without really watching it. He just let his mind go mushy for a while.

When he was done with that, Digger dialed Kevin's number. Kevin picked up, surprising him, as he had expected to leave a message.

"Hey, Kevin."

"Yes?"

"Kevin. What if it weren't about the money?"

"Look, Digger. I don't need your judgment."

"No. No. I'm just saying. What if you didn't need the money? What if you had all the money you needed, needed to go to a decent school, money to get out of this town—"

"Look, man. I've made my decision. Got it? It's all a game of musical chairs, Digger, and you'd better make quick work of finding out where you fit in in this world. You like to draw, *love* to draw, but you've said it yourself. The world no longer gives a shit about people like you."

They hung up. Digger stared out the window. He fished Mook's phone number out of his pocket and dialed it. When nobody answered, he left a message.

"Hey, Mook. This is Digger calling again. We met at the *Paint It Black* thing. Just making sure you got the tape I sent. Also, I could really use some advice. You can reach me at the RainTree Motel. Room 116. Talk to you soon. Bye." Mook wasn't gonna call Digger back. Digger knew that. People acted all chummy, made plans with you, then disappeared. Everybody thinks they're famous.

The afternoon figure workshop was smaller than usual. Activity whirled and buzzed around Digger; however, none of it seemed to graze him. He was sleepwalking through this world. He had the feeling one has when released from the hospital midday. He had no real sense of priorities.

He took a horse and straddled it. Digger did not recognize many students and did not acknowledge any whom he did. He sat with his palms on his thighs, ready, ready for something that just wasn't coming. All the world pressed flat around him like murals on painted walls. No depth. Just flat.

Digger took out a piece of charcoal and stared at it. It all seemed so absurd. He made a few marks, but there was no use. The Magic was fading. He didn't give much of a shit anymore.

He looked around him at all of the faces. Such focus. Such drive. Such love. He no longer felt any of it. Maybe it would come back. *All you need is some rest, a break*, he thought.

Digger suddenly felt foolish, as if driving on the wrong side of the street.

He packed up and left.

Digger went home, although he couldn't think of a single good reason to. He went into the backyard and stared at his childhood climbing tree. The phone rang, and Digger sprinted to answer it.

Beverly said that she felt something invisible tightening around her, squeezing her like an anaconda. An unseen hand was pushing her from behind, shoving her toward the gallows. It was all in her mind, she said, where all of her problems lay.

"Yeah, sure. I can meet you there," Digger said over the phone. He had gone home and been working on some composition ideas.

Digger got in his bus and drove.

People walked the afternoon dirt track at the Rose Bowl. These were people without regular jobs. Some jogged in shorts or sweats, but most walked.

Beverly waved at Digger at the sight of him, then started toward him.

Digger picked up his pace to a jog to meet her. They exchanged greetings.

"If you don't mind, Digger, I don't want to walk this track."

"Then why meet up here?"

"Come. Follow me."

Digger followed Beverly off the track, through some brush, onto a craggy hiking trail. They looked out of place there, her in her neat blouse and slacks, and Digger, well, looking out of place in most places.

In silence, they stomped over rocks and fallen tree trunks, ducked under heavy branches. One of the reasons she had invited Digger was that if she needed to talk, he could handle his end admirably, and if she didn't, he wouldn't force it.

They came to a small clearing, and Beverly gave a wave that signalled fatigue.

She stopped and put her hands on her hips, pacing in a small circle while panting into the sky. Digger sat on a small tree stump.

Beverly was not in the mood for idle chit-chat. She stood there, feeling the weight of her body.

"Digger, you ever want to kill yourself?" Beverly looked at Digger.

Digger was taken slightly aback. Only slightly because he was always having conversations like this with Kevin. Besides that, he felt that he and Beverly had been inching toward a … non-romantic intimacy that dissolved much of the normal societal boundaries. And, Beverly was a rather unusual person.

"Not anymore. You gonna kill yourself, Beverly?"

She answered without hesitation.

"Peter and our daughter are never coming back. I feel… I'm empty."

Digger sat with this for a moment.

"How you gonna do it?" asked Digger.

Beverly produced the small, brown bottle and showed it to Digger. All expression was wiped from his face.

"I should just take this from you," said Digger.

"But, you won't."

"Yeah, I suppose not."

Beverly looked upon Digger, took him in as though it were the way she wanted to always remember him.

After a long, late solo lunch, Beverly figured she had put this off long enough. She wrapped a scarf around her head and set to putting her husband Peter's stuff into boxes, getting it ready for whatever was next.

When the Clapton cassette was finished playing, she didn't flip it over. She kept on working at her slow, steady, robot's pace.

She thought she heard a noise outside, like someone dropping a wrench. She poked her face into the window and saw nobody there.

Hours later, Beverly went out to the backyard. The stars were out. The crickets chirped. She lowered herself onto a patio bench and closed her eyes. She took in a deep breath. The bushy, black trees undulated, ever so slowly, ever so slightly.

Accepting her fate, Beverly kissed her fingertips, blew a good-bye kiss to the house she had shared with her beloved husband and, briefly, their child, and wondered why she wasn't crying.

Beverly went back into the house and looked for her purse. She wanted the small, brown bottle, just to hold it. It gave her a sense of lightness to hold it, a sense of calm. Just to know it was there, for whatever the right time. It was always an option. When things got too much, there was always an option.

Her purse was on the kitchen table. She reached in and fished around, then felt a wave of panic. She emptied out the purse on the table and frantically sorted through its contents.

The bottle. The poison. It was gone.

Chapter 42 - Out the Door

Don, the teacher of Digger's illustration night class, had assigned an image that embodied the feeling of the Santa Monica Pier for the Santa Monica Chamber of Commerce, so Digger thought he'd head out to Santa Monica to shoot some "scrap," photo reference.

Despite it still being wintertime, there really was no off-season in Southern California.

Plenty of couples pushing strollers and strolling elders passed up and down the pier, stopping at the railing, pointing at the horizon, and smiling for photos.

Digger took out his Kodak Instamatic camera. Amid the cry of the seagulls, Digger shot the hibernating carousel, people fishing off the pier, those cleaning the fish, kids pointing at their fallen cotton candy, the dormant Ferris wheel, and the famous welcoming arch painted in blue with white letters. He'd shot two rolls and figured that was enough. He would drop them off at the one-hour photo place. (They sold ice cream by the cone there.)

Heading home, Digger was hungry; he kept his eyes peeled for something decent to fill his stomach as he drove back up Venice Blvd. *I should have brought a sack lunch*, he thought. All of the expenses added up; the lunches out, the film, the developing …

He spied "Hurry Curry." Sounded good. He pulled over and parked. Hurry Curry was a small Indian buffet place. He'd never tried Indian food before.

The man who ran the register was wrapped in a sheet-like cloth and had a small dot on his lower forehead. He greeted Digger warmly and suggested he try the mango lassi, a sweet yoghurt drink. Sure, Digger said.

Digger was furnished with a tray with a china plate. He pointed out his choices of entrees. They were placed on the plate beside a scoop of long-grained rice.

"Enjoy," said the owner, after he rang Digger up.

Digger took his tray and chose one of the empty tables.

He took a sip of the drink. It was like a thinn-ish milkshake, but tart.

Oh. My God. Where have I been all my life?

The mango lassi was incredible, like nothing he'd ever had before.

He picked up the bread. It was slightly puffy and slightly charred. The man had called it "naan." He tore off a piece and folded it, filling it with the dark green curried spinach that Digger assumed was the *palak paneer*. Digger had to close his eyes, so deep was the flavor.

The whole meal was just astounding, the tandoori chicken, the potato cauliflower curry… everything.

I never want to eat anything else again.

The owner stood at the register, watching Digger finish his meal, with an eager face.

Digger wiped his mouth with a paper napkin and gave the universal hand signal for "okay."

The owner was visibly pleased. Digger got up to leave.

"You will please come again!"

"Count on it!"

Digger encountered a parking meter that had already gone red. Luckily, he hadn't gotten a ticket yet.

Heading back up Venice, Digger saw a sign that he just couldn't pass up.

The Army Surplus Store was a wonderland of fascinating stuff, the uses of which were largely a mystery to Digger. There were field jackets like Kevin's, complete battle dress uniforms, sleeping bags, gas masks, metal ammo cases... all in Army green.

He picked up what looked like a cross between a shovel and a folding knife.

"That's an E-Tool. E stands for entrenching. You use that for digging in hard dirt around your tent," volunteered a bearded, large-chested man in a hunting vest.

"Uh, thanks. What's this? asked Digger.

"That there is a HazMat suit, for the handling or transport of hazardous or dangerous materials. Comes with headgear and gloves. Keep you nice and safe."

"What do you get for something like this?"

"Tell you what. I'll give you that bad boy for $65, out the door."

"Hmmm." Digger weighed it in his arms.

"Make it fifty, cash, and it's yours, kid."

Chapter 43 - Candles and Linens. Hobnobbin'!

It was an intimate private dinner party. Candles and linens. Hobnobbin'!

His table manners were good enough, but when the conversation swirled around young Dean, it never seemed to whisk him along. He didn't laugh when they did, and laughed when they did not. They rattled off names he didn't recognize and talked of places that one simply *must* go.

In attendance were Lauren, an NPR journalist, and her partner, Siobhan. Robert, an art columnist, and his wife Beth, and their hosts, Dennis and Peggy, were a patron of the arts power couple.

Dean no longer waited for the host to replenish his drink. In fact, he was done being invisible altogether.

"There is just as much solid draftsmanship in comics than in any current fine art," asserted Dean, apropos of nothing.

"But I totally agree with you, Dean," implored Robert. "The schools and the marketplace have now turned their backs on the most basic of skills. Why, you should see the student work of the '50s. The Design Center's first term head studies in gouache were something most graduates can't do today."

"But, fine art and illustration has changed," said Dini Topp. "No longer are we using the same old tired traditions. Norman Rockwell?"

Dini Topp made a loud snoring noise. "We have moved into new and exciting directions. The students of today are the elite, shunning the tired baggage of the past."

"Hey! Whose side are you on?" Dean felt naked, betrayed by his lover and mentor.

Lauren squirmed uneasily in her seat, while Siobhan seemed to enjoy the show. Dennis and Peggy looked like a wrestling tag team, just waiting to be tapped in.

"I'm not on anybody's side, Dean. Dean, you've had enough to drink."

"Oh yeah?" Dean's head felt hot, but he thought he was still in control. "You've had enough to eat." Dean leaned back in his chair and took an exaggerated look at Dini Topp's supple midsection.

Dini Topp leaned close and hissed in Dean's ear.

"You will not embarrass me nor yourself in front of my friends!" She then snarled, "We will *finish* this when we get home."

Finish. It was the way she said *finish*. *She's through with me*, thought Dean. Oh yeah? He'd beat her to the punch.

"I'll tell you, some things don't need updating," Dean said, then looked at Dini Topp. "Some things do."

They left the party without lingering and hurried to Dini Topp's car.

"Proud of yourself?" asked Dini Topp, strangling the steering wheel of her BMW.

Dean sat slumped in his seat, sulking.

"You know, you're shooting yourself in the foot to spite your foot."

Dean hated her sometimes. Times like now.

Chapter 44 - Allergies

Digger was getting ready to leave the house to meet his mother for dinner. He looked over the calendar on the wall. Valentine's Day was approaching fast. Valentine's Day. Beverly's wedding anniversary.

He drove the short distance to the Carrows and parked near the door. He entered and scanned the room. His mother was already seated and waiting for him.

Karen gave menus to Digger and his mom as soon as he sat down.

"My son, here, is taking me out to dinner to celebrate his going to a fancy art academy."

"Oh, he's a regular here. Congrats." Karen gave Digger a wink.

Digger made a half-smile of thanks. Mother's skin was pale. She looked ill. Dark circles hung from her eyes.

"Be right back with your drinks." Karen then went away to place their order.

"Digger, are you sleeping with that woman?" asked Mother.

"Mother, I've decided not to attend Design Center."

"I knew it! Once again, throwing away your talent. If I had half your talent, I'd be rich by now. No! I'm not going to be negative."

Karen returned with their beverages, then began to take their orders.

"I'll have the pasta with Thai sauce," ordered Digger.

"What's in that? You know I'm allergic to nuts."

"The peanuts are ground into the sauce," informed Karen.

"Different sauce, then. No peanuts. I'm allergic to peanuts," insisted mother.

It puzzled Karen that this woman should demand changing someone else's order.

"Just substitute the alfredo sauce," smiled the mother.

Karen smiled warmly at Digger. Mother noticed this.

"You should *never* date a man," mother addressed Karen, "who is bad to his mother." She then returned her gaze to Digger.

Waitress Karen looked as though she had just stepped in something vile. She left the table with their orders.

A short while later, Karen brought their food. They dug in. Mother kept eating off Digger's plate. She slurped up the noodles loudly as they slapped her in the face.

"Mmmm. Mmmmm. Mmmmm. Why is my food never as good as what you order?"

She was eating much too fast. She was gulping down shrimp.

Mother coughed. She began to choke.

"Wait! Is this Alfredo sauce? Digger. Did you poison me? Tastes like poison."

Digger let the question hang in the air for a moment.

"Nobody poisoned you, mother."

Mother began to breathe loudly, laboriously. She reached for her water.

Digger stood and rounded the table. He took his mother around the waist, ready to give her the Heimlich.

I could let her die, Digger thought. *I could just hold her, for appearances, and just let her die.* She was clawing for air. He thought of what Audrey had said. He thought about the past.

He pulled in one great yank, ejecting the offending food from her throat. It was a large shrimp.

"Excuse me? Karen? I think my mother's having trouble. Could you please call 911? And, the check, please."

Yes, Valentine's Day was approaching. Beverly had been through a lot. She was Digger's new best friend. She deserved a Valentine. Something special. And, Digger knew just what.

Chapter 45 - Cool Like That

Covina Chevrolet was having a big tent sale. It was in the paper. Free hot dogs! Soda! Clowns! Balloons for the kids! This Saturday and Sunday!

Karen strolled the grassy lawn in front of the police station. It was catty-corner from the main dealership. They let the Chevy dealer use it for the sale, for a tidy little fee, no doubt. She fanned herself with her newspaper, eating a hot dog and slurping a Dr. Pepper. The California winter sun was burning a hole in the back of her ski parka.

She wandered under one of the white tents full of brand-new parked show cars.

Ooh. She liked this one.

"1985 Caprice Classic. I drive one, m'self." The salesman slid in out of nowhere. He wore a moustache. Kinda cute, like Barney Miller.

"Mmmm… Black like a limo," said Karen.

"That's right."

After about half an hour, she returned to the hot dog table with a balloon in tow and asked for a couple more dogs, to which the salesman behind the table said, "One to a customer, lady. You've had enough."

"Ah, yes." With that, Karen left his company. She returned not three minutes later with Barney Miller.

"Seth, you give this beautiful lady all the hot dogs she wants while I write up her new black Caprice Classic." Barney Miller looked at Karen with a wink. "Black like a limo. All cash."

Seth didn't seem all that pleased to accommodate.

"Yes, and I'd like extra mustard, Seth, *S'il vous plaît,*" said Karen.

*

That night, Karen picked Maria up at her apartment in her brand new car.

She pulled up to where Maria was waiting, standing on the curb. Maria climbed in.

"Oh, my god! It's like a limo!" shrieked Maria.

"Didn't I tell you?"

"How did you afford it?"

Karen took a moment. Maria was a good friend, close.

"Been scrimping and saving my tips, y'know? Got $1,200 trade-in on my old Civic!"

"Nice!"

"So it's time to celebrate!"

"That's why I took the night off!"

The ladies erupted in a *Whoo-hoo*!

"By the way, tonight is my treat. I do hope Rudolpho is dancing tonight."

"What'd you do, Karen? Rob a bank?"

"Well… maybe not a *bank*…" They popped in a Julio Iglesias tape and laughed uproariously as they drove away.

*

Levi watched his son, Sherman, do his homework at the dinner table. There were textbooks, workbooks, notebooks, and comic books splayed across the table, leaving little room for anything else.

"Could I draw now, pop?"

"After you finish your homework."

Sherman returned to his study without complaint. He was a good kid.

Sherman tapped his thumb with each finger on his right hand before picking his pencil back up and scribbling in his workbook. Levi left the kitchen and headed for his bedroom.

Certain that he did this unobserved, Levi carefully placed a large wad of large bills, bound with a rubber band, into a coffee can. He then placed the coffee can upon the upper shelf in his closet.

Levi took a large hardback book off his bed and opened it. The inscription read, "ALL YOU'LL EVER NEED! -D."

He closed the book to reveal its title, "HOW TO DRAW COMICS THE MARVEL WAY." Digger had told Levi how much this book had meant to him as a young boy, just starting out. *It's an art school in a book*! Digger had told Levi.

"I'm done with my homework, pop!" Sherman yelled from the other side of the tiny house.

Levi rejoined his son in the small dining room.

"Sherman. A friend of mine sent you a present."

"A present? For me?"

"Yeah, this guy likes giving presents," Levi smiled. "He's cool like that."

Chapter 46 – Blackout...I Am Really Going to Enjoy This

Dean's dark apartment only allowed a slight rim lighting to describe its contents—its loft railings, its staircase, its vast bookshelves, and easels. All of these are mere hints of objects standing in the cool darkness lit by leaking sunlight. It must have been well past noon.

He tried lifting his head. Oof! It was heavy. *Where am I?* he wondered. His mind swam against powerful currents of memory undertow. Liquor bottles stood on the coffee table like a gleaming glass city.

He was used to being the biggest fish in the pond. Now, he felt as though all the other fish were swimming past him, and he just could not keep up.

Digger came to his sloshy mind. Digger was far past him, and there was a whole ocean of Diggers out there, guys who could outdraw him without even noticing him. He wanted to hate Digger. He wanted to hate Digger so bad.

Dean thought he'd had it made when Dini Topp had taken him for a lover. The schoolboy fantasy of banging the teacher had given him an extra inch in height. Add to this the prospect of her being his entreé into the *fast lane*. It was too rich. It was a dream come true.

But now, he was emerging as a joke. He was the worst kind of joke, a cliché. The failed artist.

He fell backward into an abyss of sadness and hopelessness.

Dean fumbled with a bottle of vodka before chugging the last of its contents, then he passed out on the huge sectional leather sofa.

The doorbell rang.

*

Dini Topp was pissed. She was supposed to meet Dean at his place. She had tried to call to reschedule, but he wasn't answering his phone, nor was his answering machine picking up. She needed him to bring her a large file she had left at his place. *Damn it.*

She looked in her rear view mirror with the feeling that she was being followed, but shook it off.

Dini Topp took the elevator up to Dean's floor and thought she heard footsteps on the stairs. They weren't ordinary footsteps. They were running footsteps. Running? Upstairs?

"More power to ya', pal," she said aloud, as she exited the elevator car.

She got to Dean's door and rang the doorbell.

"Aw, to hell with it." She opened the door, using the key Dean had made for her.

All of a sudden, she felt herself shoved violently from behind into the apartment, landing on her hands and knees. Before she could even make a sound, a moist rag covered her muzzle, and she passed out.

The drapes that covered the gigantic windows in Dean's Brewery loft studio were only partially closed, letting in an enormous blast of setting sun.

When she came to, she was weak and woozy. Her vision was all stretched and smeary.

She lay on her back with the rag still covering her nose and mouth. She removed it and made a small groan. That's when the sounds stopped. The sounds of someone tinkering stopped, and Dini Topp froze.

A face appeared before her. When speech again found her, she said, "You. Beverly's friend. Doggie."

"Close enough. Let's get you off the floor," Digger offered.

"Yes. Yes, off of the floor."

Digger helped Dini Topp to her rubbery feet and led her to the long and thick wooden dining room table. It had been cleared of everything.

He laid Dini Topp on the table and shoved a clean rag in her mouth. Then, he lifted into the air a nail gun.

"Hey, look what I found in Dean's studio." With that, Digger fastened her hands, palms down, to the wooden table, with two carpenters' nails each, meant to penetrate concrete. Dini Topp let out a muffled scream. "Dean!" she cried out.

"Sorry. But your striking Viking is blackout drunk. Here, let me show you.

Digger went to the kitchen sink and filled a large spaghetti pot with water. He then brought it over to Dean, who lay passed out on the sofa. He doused Dean with the cold water. Dean didn't move an inch. Digger slapped him across the face, hard. That left a red mark against his chalk white skin. Dean didn't budge.

Dini Topp screamed again, if not continuously, so great was the burning pain, shooting through her crushed hands. Digger secured the rag in her mouth by tying a gag around her head.

Laid out on one of Dean's art trolleys was a scary and elaborate arsenal of tools; surplus store dental and surgical tools, X-Acto knives, razor blades as well as large anatomy texts. One was by Leonardo Da Vinci, whose studies were works of art in themselves.

"You know, a blackout drunk can sometimes not remember what he, or she, did for hours or even days before. They can do the most horrendous things without remembering one bit of it? They can drive places, shoot games of pool, and beat someone nearly to death after having a two-hour conversation with them. Did you know that? Oh, my mother knows that. That's because, among other things, my father was (is?) a blackout drunk. Not one person in my nuclear family went unscathed by that. Hell, my mother gave me my first broken nose. Merry Christmas!"

Digger looked out at the expansive and expensive view of the Los Angeles skyline.

"I really hate this place. The people are stupid, no one has any manners, and a lot of people are just mean," spoke Digger, softly.

Dini Topp was screaming herself hoarse.

Digger then picked up a large, expensive and gorgeously bound book on human anatomy. The books all came from Dean's well-stocked shelves.

Digger took his eyes off the book and bore them into those of his captive.

"I don't like you," he said. "You're mean, you're rude, and you're stupid." Digger neared the face of his squirming guest. "Three strikes. You're out."

"I gotta admit," said Digger, holding up a coil of cotton rope, "your boyfriend sure has *everything*. You know, I really lucked out. Who'd have known you'd wind up here, with Dean, well... incapacitated. I guess it's my lucky day."

He went on to tie up Dini Topp tightly.

"Scream all you like. You must already know that Dean liked to brag about the soundproof quality of these concrete loft apartments."

Digger spread plastic tarps all over the floor, then went to the large, industrial sink and washed his hands up to the elbows, like a surgeon. He then stepped into a rubberized HazMat suit and donned a pair of nitrile surgical gloves.

"I hated you the moment I met you. But now, by being such a complete *ass*, you've volunteered for *this.*" Digger gestured around him like a presenter at a car show. "As good old Mom used to say, you go sticking your hand into cages, kid, and sometime you're going to pull out a bloody stump." Digger placed a surgical cap on his head.

"Yes, I hate you. But what's worse for you is that Beverly hates you. And Valentine's Day is right around the corner. Oh, did you hear that? I almost said *around the coroner!*" Digger gave an exaggerated chuckle. The big ham.

"This has been a long time coming. Yes, you ought to make a perfect Valentine. It's just a bonus that your job will now be open."

The body on the table struggled. Digger picked up an X-Acto knife. It gleamed in the golden light of Magic Hour.

"You're not gonna need those eyelids," informed Digger. Dini Topp screamed, straining her vocal cords bloody.

Digger propped the book up on a cookbook holder.

"Just know this, kiddo. I am really, really going to enjoy this."

Chapter 47 - Waking Up is Hard to Do (or Bad Wake Up)

Slowly. Ever so slowly. And *painfully*. Dean began to emerge from unconsciousness. His head felt like an anvil and was equally difficult to raise. Through one squinting eye, he tried to get his bearings. *Where am I?*

He was drenched in what had to be more than sweat. It had been like somebody had poured a bucket of water on him. *Okay, I'm on the couch.*

There was a welt on his cheek. He felt it. What the hell had transpired and for how long?

The air had a strange stench hanging in it, coppery, not unlike fresh road kill. The smell wasn't faint. It was powerful.

It was too painful to investigate right now. Dean just closed his eyes and let his head fall back until, *What the hell?*

He bolted upright and looked around him. His easels and trolleys had been moved from their usual stations... and that *smell*.

With all his might, he rocked himself out of the sofa and into a standing position, which made his back crack loudly. He must have been lying in that position for hours. As his eyes adjusted to the darkness, he stumbled toward a light switch.

He flicked a switch and moved a slider, then voila! Let there be light. He checked his Hugo Boss watch. It was just after 11pm. His eyes were caught by the sight of the bloody trolley, with all of its gooey tools. His gaze then moved to the table where, *oh, my god*! There was Dini Topp. At least just about enough parts to *make* a Dini Topp. He recognized the white cashmere sweater and blonde doll hair. The rest of it was a display of neatly organized parts.

Dean screamed. He screamed like he'd been given a haircut with a chainsaw. He fell backward onto the floor, where he landed on his bottom, immediately scooting in the opposite direction of the flayed and mutilated meat and bone that, technically, comprised a corpse.

Dean panicked. *What to do? What to do?*

He couldn't call the police. Not until he remembered what he did during his blackout.

Think, think, think.

The gruesome tableau vivant snagged his eye and jerked him into a vomiting fit.

He scrambled to the bathroom, stripping to the waist and leaving his shirt on the floor. He continued to vomit in the toilet, all the time wailing. Whatever his feelings for Dini Topp, they were being scrambled right now with the prospect that he might have killed her in a drunken stupor.

Dean removed the rest of his clothing and crawled into the shower. He could not feel the hot or cold. He just stood there, expressionless. Suddenly, he jolted into action, scrubbing his entire body with an apricot scrub that contained crushed walnut shells. Without thinking, he scrubbed it into his long blond hair. When he was finished, he hadn't even fully rinsed it out.

He put on a new pair of black jeans and a t-shirt.

Dean sat on the edge of his bed and stared at his cordless phone. Then, summoning up as much courage as he could muster, he made the call he truly most dreaded.

He called his father.

Chapter 48 - Breaking News!

Digger's sister Audrey turned on the TV. It was time for the morning "Little House on the Prairie" reruns, but a montage of interviewees talked straight to the camera.

"That guy's hardcore. Sick," said a random art student.

"He's an artist. A true artist," said Jean.

"Doesn't surprise me a bit," Rachel said.

"He'd throw these parties. He'd get. So. Drunk," Library Girl.

"I suppose I did notice something of a temper in class," Don O'Conner, the teacher, said.

"Whoa. I'm just like. Whoa. He was wild. He would wave this *gun* around." Tony said.

"He's my classmate. He's a staunch and unapologetic advocate of tradition and the craft of draughtsmanship. I don't believe he could have ever done this." Digger said.

*

Beverly took her General Foods International Coffee to the back patio along with her leather folder. She turned on a portable radio, set to NPR. Terry Gross was interviewing somebody or another.

She opened the folder and took out the pen inside. Blankly staring at the yellow legal pad, she clicked the pen repeatedly. She seemed to remember that if it were handwritten and signed and dated, in ink, then it served as a legal will.

Beverly really didn't have many folks to leave anything to, and leaving all to Patsy seemed like gifting her nothing but the hassle of sorting through piles of stuff for the Goodwill.

Suddenly, the local news break hit her like a bucket of ice water.

Apparently, somebody had killed the Admissions Director at Design Center.

Dini Topp was dead.

After the initial shock of the news subsided, Beverly realized that she really wasn't sorry. In fact, (sip) she was fine with the whole thing. Dini Topp was dead? There were a lot of people whom she would miss more.

Beverly immediately wanted to call Digger, find out if he'd heard the news.

She dialed his number. She got the mother. She left a message.

*

The calamitous sounds of hammering and drilling drowned out the radio. Bridget was using the circular saw to cut two-by-fours down to size. "Antigone" opened in a week and a half, and the sets were being revised as they were being built. What a hassle.

Lunchtime came, and all noise dropped to a low milling.

Bridget's new boyfriend showed up, bearing two pastrami sandwiches. He kissed her as he sat down on the sawdust next to her.

Things were going well. Bridget wouldn't say that life was perfect, but she sure felt good.

The radio announced the murder of a local art school administrator. For some reason, Digger came to mind. He was taking classes at an art school.

She liked his weird little— or big, shall we say— brain. She missed him.

*

The interrogation room was warm, and the light was low. It came from overhead, casting ghoulish shadows down Dean's Scandinavian good looks. He was jittery in his seat. No windows.

There were two men, although only one spoke. The other gave Dean the very real impression that he was going to beat him to death.

"Did you *expect* a visit from Dini Topp that afternoon?" asked Mister Talk.

"No. I did not." Dean was trying to play it cool. "I want to see a lawyer."

"If you didn't do this, then who did?" The man's spittle got in Dean's eyes.

"I have no fuckin' idea. Some fucking psycho." Dean began to weep. He began to cry. This was all just too much.

"Some careful psycho fuck who hates you and wants to frame you, maybe?" asked the interrogator.

"Yeah!" Dean ran through every face he knew, like the spinning wheel on *The Price is Right*. He had absolutely no idea who he had ever met who could do this. It had to be a stranger, some random stranger.

"Give me a fucking break, Dean. You did it. You killed your girlfriend because she embarrassed you—she embarrassed you at that dinner party, she embarrassed you at the fancy art chateau—"

"Design Center."

"Whatever the fuck. You did it because you hate women and you hate yourself. You're a blackout drunk who does fucked up shit when he drinks, then conveniently doesn't remember a thing."

Dean thrashed his head *no,* straining against the handcuffs and leg irons.

"You know who thrashes around like that? Guys with guilty consciences."

*

At the police station, Dean's father, a salt-and-pepper, cuff-linked executive, talked to the squarish and leathery detective.

"Why are you so quick to conclude that it's my son?"

"Sir, Dini Topp has been found murdered and mutilated in your son's art studio. Your son was found covered in her blood. All witnesses paint your son as angry, morbid, and violent, as well as a dipshit, blackout booze hound. Just because he made the call to us doesn't mean he didn't do it."

On a table, oozy and glossy crime scene photos lay, so gruesome that one would swear they emitted an actual stench.

"The whole place looks like a medieval, like a" —the detective stammered, scrambling for the words— "butcher college. Anatomy textbooks lay open all over the place.

"We found a gun. I've been doing this job for twenty-one years. And frankly, when we questioned him, your boy sounded like somebody with something to hide. He might be a tough guy when he's got a lady tied up so that she can't move her head, arms, or legs, but that kid ain't gonna last five minutes on the witness stand, let alone the singles' scene of State Prison."

"Sounds like the DA either wants to look tough on crime or just has a hard-on for rich kids."

The detective stared at the father with what might have been disgust. There was no point to being in this room any longer, so the detective left.

Dean's father paced the waiting room, straining to get a seemingly impossible kink out of his neck. He was taken to a small and stuffy room, painted a nauseating grey-green.

It had a couple of metal chairs and a small rectangular metal table. No windows.

The door banged open, and Dean was brought in wearing handcuffs and leg irons. The barrel-chested officer who had brought him into the room chained Dean to the table, then stood guard in the corner, just in case Dean wanted to kill anybody else in here.

Dean's father looked more annoyed and angry than concerned or protective. Perhaps all of this had made the man miss a meeting.

"I didn't do it. I didn't do anything."

Dean's father locked eyes with his son. "What did you do? You did something."

"Honestly, Dad! I didn't do anything!"

"Like when you *didn't* steal a few grand from my safe and blow it all, impressing your idiot friends? Like when you *didn't* try to sell one of my Jaguars behind my back? Like you *didn't* assault that girl and get your drunken ass kicked out of that school over a year ago?"

"I swear. I didn't do this."

Dean's father folded his arms and looked at his son, as if trying to decide whether or not to buy him at auction.

"Dean, I want to believe you, but I'm having quite a bit of trouble. I want to take you at your word."

"Then, put some of that beloved money to use and get me the fuck out of here!"

Chapter 49 - Tying Up Loose Ends

Digger entered the liquor store wearing a baseball cap pulled down low. The store was miles away from his usual stomping grounds. He strolled the aisles, looking at the candy bars, bags of chips, and cans of Spaghetti-Os. There was a carousel of greeting cards.

He noted the security camera in the corner and turned his back, hunching his shoulders.

Digger considered making a decoy purchase, some beef jerky, and a magazine, but finally realized that that would be foolish. His real motive would be transparent enough.

He approached the man at the counter. The man looked at him like an inconvenience.

"I'd like a couple of bottles of Jack Daniels, please," asked Digger. "That one there."

"The quarter-pint."

"And... two of the minis."

The man reached the crammed shelf behind him, retrieving the items. He then placed them into a small paper bag.

"Okay, let's see some ID," the man asked Digger. He looked ready to return the bottles to the shelf at a moment's notice.

Digger opened his tattered wallet and slid three one-hundred-dollar bills toward the cashier.

"There you go. Three forms of ID."

A couple of days later, Digger was driving home in the late afternoon when he saw the truck. There were the AC/DC and Jack Daniels stickers as well as the familiar-looking license plate number. It was parked at the local Spend-Rite supermarket. Digger turned into the parking lot.

He circled around a couple of times to find out if he could see the tough guy owner inside the store and to see if the truck's windows were rolled down.

Good news on both counts. Mr. Tough Guy must have been deep in the store and left his windows down. Digger called to mind the beating he took at the hands of this thug, how this bully destroyed, soaked his nearly completed sketchbook in urine.

Digger parked his VW bus behind the Fotomat, maybe twenty yards from the asshole's truck. He trotted the two aisles over, wearing his "disguise" cap pulled down low.

As he neared the truck, a police cruiser rolled by. Digger returned the cop's eye contact with a tip of the hat, and the policeman just went on his way.

Digger had both the half-pint and a mini of Jack Daniels in his jacket pockets. Feverishly, he tried to decide which to use.

Aw hell. When he reached the truck, he quickly wiped both bottles down for fingerprints with a bandana and gently tossed the bottles through the truck's open window. He could hear the smaller bottle roll onto the floor and under the seat.

Digger then jogged away in the opposite direction from his VW bus. He would come back for it later.

*

About ten minutes later, Tough Guy emerged from the automatic doors of the Spend-Rite, carrying a brown paper bag full of groceries.

He opened the door to the cab of the truck and moved the bottle of whiskey out of the way to make room for the bag.

Wait a minute. He didn't remember leaving a bottle of Jack on the front seat. *Oh well.* He was pleased with his good fortune.

Tough Guy took the driver's seat and turned the key in his ignition, and the radio came to life. It was tuned to a rock station. They were playing Blue Öyster Cult's *Don't Fear the Reaper*.

He banged his fingers against the steering wheel to the music.

Tough Guy pulled out of the parking lot. He thought he had recognized that VW bus from somewhere. He shrugged.

He headed for his girlfriend's house. She was expecting him, him, and the food.

When he reached there, he parked in the driveway behind her mini-truck, where he cut the engine.

He spun the top off the bottle of Jack and took a huge swig. Felt great.

His girlfriend, the one from the night of Digger's beating at Carrow's, emerged from the house to greet him. Suddenly, he knit his brow. He grew hot. His throat felt scratchy and constricted. He fought for breath. He involuntarily stomped his feet. He grabbed the steering wheel and turned it back and forth frantically.

His girlfriend screamed. She ran around to the driver's side door and yanked it open.

Tough Guy gagged. He choked. He reached. He flailed. He fell to the side until… he died.

The girlfriend held him as she wailed.

*

Digger came home to find that his mom had all of his stuff in boxes in the living room. They were piled up like at the balloon factory. She was closing the last of them with a tape dispenser when he entered.

"Watch what you wish for, kiddo," she said, wiping her forehead with her forearm. "You want to be Johnny Grown-Up, then be Johnny Grown-up."

He had no doubt that the boxes were stuffed with now broken piles of his unsorted property.

She asked Digger for his keys, and he gave them over.

Digger carried all of the boxes to the curb.

"That's where the trash goes," she said as if he had put down a glass without a coaster. "You're gonna put it there? Why don't you put it in that van of yours?"

"I'll send for it," he lied.

"What about your bed, your furniture?"

"Sell it."

Digger's mother just stood there, taking him in. This is the young man to whom she gave birth eighteen short years ago. Now, here he stood, six feet of pain in the ass genius. She congratulated herself on the job she did raising him.

She then took him in a fierce, yet awkward embrace. She had heard that suicidal people often gave or threw away all of their belongings.

Nah, Digger wouldn't do that.

"I love you, my son, my son. You're not a bad kid." She tousled Digger's hair. "You just got a stupid streak."

Digger pushed away to arm's length from his mother. He looked at her as if measuring her features.

"Goodbye, mother."

"It's not *goodbye*, Digger. We'll all still be around."

She waved as Digger pulled away.

"Make sure to give us your new number when you get one!"

Chapter 50 - Murmurs and Whispers

The afternoon figure workshop was jam-packed with students. The lithe and willowy model stood on the podium, waiting for a lull in the tumult to ask if anybody wished to begin.

Beverly entered. The sheer number of people made her bump into a standstill.

There were murmurs and whispers bubbling. *Did you hear about that guy, Dean? I heard he killed some lady in admissions. I heard they were sleeping together...* That sort of thing.

She looked around for Digger. No dice. Maybe Pashone would know.

Beverly looked around, waited, then finally asked the willowy model if she knew if Pashone was coming today. The model shrugged. Beverly scrunched her mouth to one side.

Beverly looked for Tony, Rachel, and Jonny. She spotted Rachel, sharpening her charcoal pencil with a razor blade, standing over a trash can.

When she pushed her way through to Rachel, she bumped into Tony, who was also approaching the trash can. He had no pencil to sharpen. He seemed to just be there to steep in the zeitgeist.

"Man! Did you hear about Dean?" said Tony. "That is fucked! Up!'

"That guy was such an orifice," said Rachel, chewing a wad of grape bubble gum.

"Have either of you seen Digger?" asked Beverly.

"Nah. Maybe he's with Jonny."

The model shouted above the din that she was going to start the first group of poses. This announcement immediately sent half of the room's occupants out, and the other half straddling their wooden horses and stewarding their easels.

Beverly joined the exodus.

*

Digger tried Beverly's back doorknob. It was locked—she usually left it unlocked—so he climbed to the second story and shimmied in through an open bathroom window.

He had no idea how long she would be gone, so he had to be efficient.

Digger tiptoed from the bathroom and through the bedroom to her small upstairs office.

It was an orderly little workspace. Luckily, Beverly was organized. Everything was fairly easy to find. He had some loose ends to tie up, and Beverly was one of them. Her file cabinet was built into her desk, right next to the safe.

Digger grabbed all he needed and then headed downstairs for the front door. He heard a sound that made him freeze halfway down the stairs. He listened.

It was the mailman delivering the mail. He shoved it noisily through the small metal door that banged shut, then he walked away.

Digger didn't want to run the risk of being spotted leaving out the front door. Who knew when Beverly would be back, so Digger made his way back up the stairs, through the bedroom, and to the bathroom, where he wiggled through the window out.

*

Beverly stood next to her car in the waning sunlight. Suddenly, she had the oddest feeling about Digger, as if his warmth were gone. As if he had died. She shuddered and realized that she was just being ridiculous.

She pulled the door open and climbed in.

Beverly might give him a call later in the evening. Maybe he'd be up for babysitting a middle-aged woman who had homework to complete, and a past to bury.

She was grateful for Digger. He kept her from getting too lonely. He needed her, a young man, learning about the world.

She could cook a simple dinner. *It's important to have things to look forward to.*

Chapter 51 - You Know Who Did It, Don't You?

Damn it. Digger had forgotten something important in his closet. Maybe Audrey hadn't left for her shift at Hot Dog on a Stick yet.

He drove back to the house. He had a phone message. It was written on a scrap of paper torn off a scroll that was mounted on the kitchen wall next to the avocado green telephone. Digger had to squint to make out his mother's writing. It read, *Pet Pan something,* then a phone number.

He called his mother up at the real estate office. Luckily, she had "floor time," which meant that she wasn't out showing properties.

"I told you not to bother me at work, Digger."

"I can't read this message that you left."

"Well, what does it say?" she asked, exasperated.

"It says that you flunked penmanship in school."

"I'm hanging up."

"Wait! Wait. It looks like it says, *Pet Pan something.* "

"Oh, right! It says to call Detective Dan. Detective Dan Lorca. He's a cop." Digger could hear her smiling over the phone. "Digger. What did you do?"

Digger, recognized a shapely Design Center student as she passed by him on his way into the police station. She was a full-timer. *A fine art major,* he thought. She made him want to tie her up.

He checked his watch. 3:00. He had a 3:15 appointment.

The large room was not as bustling as Digger expected. Digger's name was called.

Two detectives took Digger into an office. Nothing sinister. Just some photos and certificates on the wall, a standing American flag…

"Thanks for coming in, mister—"

"Call me Digger. Everybody does." Digger was trying to recall everything he'd ever seen on TV about forensics experts. *Don't lie. Calm. Calm. Don't lie.*

The two cops laughed.

"Okay! Digger it is."

They offered him a beverage. He politely declined.

Detective Dan had a partner who stood in the corner with his arms crossed.

"So, you actually took a class with him," asked the detective.

"With Dean? That's right."

"Do you think he killed her?"

Boy, Digger thought, *they're going right for it.*

"Like I said before to the news guys, I don't think Dean is capable of such an act."

"Wow. You are quite the friend. Quite the friend."

Oh shit. Are they going to try to pin me as an accomplice? Had I been spotted by one of Dean's neighbors? Would they be able to identify me for certain?

"Too bad, he doesn't feel the same way," continued the detective.

Detective Dan showed Digger a sketchbook.

"This is Dean's. It's not just a sketchbook. It has entries, like a diary." Dan flipped the book open. "You're in here, Digger. A *lot*."

Digger pursued the pages.

"You and some other students. Something of an enemies list," suggested Detective Dan. "He was a pretty jealous guy."

"Envious, you say?"

"We're thinking that if this rich kid makes bail, that you might be in danger."

Digger couldn't believe his ears.

"Don't worry, Digger. We'll keep a close eye on you."

Digger trotted down the steps of the police station. On his way to the metered parking, he spotted Rachel and Tony and made his way over to them. Rachel smiled warmly at Digger as a greeting.

He was under police surveillance for all he knew. The last thing in the world he wanted right now was to be recognized. He wanted to be alone, alone to cope, to freak out, to fall apart.

"Did they interrogate you, too? That was so rad," began Tony. "I mean, it's a tragedy. We all are aware of how tragic it all is, but being interrogated is pretty rad. You gotta admit."

"I," Digger deadpanned, "admit nothing."

"Fuck. I can't believe they killed Dini Topp."

"I can believe it," said Rachel.

*

Digger got up in the middle of the night with his mind racing. His motel room was suffocating him. He opened the window.

Digger never had an easy time getting sleep. Now, however, whatever sleep did come was light at best. He was plagued, not by guilt, but by something as relentless, fugitive fear. His mind spun relentlessly, playing and replaying scenarios, crunching and re-crunching the numbers. He was an art forger, a con artist, and a sadistic double-murderer. And it all had come so remarkably easily, so naturally.

He couldn't go into deep hiding. That would just glow with suspicion. He had to continue whatever schedule he had been keeping. But, hadn't he recently burned all of his bridges? It sure felt that way. That's probably the way it needed to be.

His head hurt. He was exhausted. He was desperate. He prayed for sleep. He prayed for an answer. He didn't know if he believed in God, but he sure wasn't going to let that get in the way.

Something in Digger cracked open, broke … like a tree struck by lightning.

I can't live like this, always looking over my shoulder. I just have to say, fuck it.

Right now, I really can't control whether I get caught or not. I've done my very best. I'll do my very best, but it's out of my hands now. I have to live like a dead man, not a man afraid of dying.

Chapter 52 - Onward

At Beverly's house, a large gift envelope had arrived. It was the kind you'd find at a mall; shiny, made of Mylar, and covered in hearts. Her heart stopped. Could it be from Peter? She opened the package slowly, trying to keep calm.

It contained a large red paper heart, rimmed with lace, atop a small sheaf of papers bound with a small binder clip. The Valentine had no writing on it, no inscription. Beverly had a secret admirer.

The top page of the stack was a letter, typewritten to Rick Jansen.

She scanned down. The letter's typed signature read her own full name. This made her eyes jump. She read the letter aloud:

To Richard Jansen, Dept. Chair, Humanities and Academics at Design Center.

Dear Richard, I appreciate the passion that is Design Center, in helping tomorrow's artists

start off with a solid base of academic training and exposure. My husband and I have been nothing but proud of the institution and I have been nothing but proud of my husband's involvement with the institution.

I, as well, would like to contribute in any way I can. I've enclosed my resume, credentials, transcripts and letters of recommendation in the hopes that you will keep me in mind to serve in any capacity, in any way you might need.

Thank you, in advance, for your valuable time and for any consideration you might afford me.

Sincerely yours, Beverly Eaton.

An arrow-shaped Post-it was stuck to the bottom of the letter, instructing her to
"Sign Here >."
There was also a large, stamped envelope, addressed to Design Center with Beverly's as the return address.
She was going to take Dini Topp's job.
The phone rang. Beverly answered. It was the auto shop.
The voice of the mechanic competed with the background noise created by power tools and hydraulic lifts. He was nearly yelling.
"Yes, Ma'am. I remember. But your car's not leaking oil. Not anymore. No. I didn't do a thing to it. You don't owe me a dime. You can pick it up anytime. Uh-huh. Bye now."
Beverly hung up the phone, puzzled, then saw something out her window. She was now bewildered. No, shocked. She steeled herself, as if there were any effective way to prepare oneself for something like this.
Through the large window, she saw her husband Peter's car pull up the driveway. Was he coming back to her, or merely here to collect his belongings?

She felt like she had been struck. Her head was woozy. Feelings that had recently refused to surface, now flooded her off her feet. She couldn't bear an answer. She couldn't bear not to know.

Beverly moved to the door and rested her hand on the knob. She stood still and took a deep breath. Her hand was shaking.

Peter, a lean man in his late thirties, wearing khakis and bearing a leather satchel slung across his body, took the smooth stone walkway to the front door.

*

In Pashone's home studio, the tables and easels were caked with a half-century of paint drippings and splotches. Jars of turpentine, varnishes, and artists' oils made a cityscape of the large table. A dusty skylight was the only source of light.

Conté sketches showed the composition of the painting series in progress on the easels. Pashone pressed play on a boom box, and the horns of Hummel shot out of its speakers.

He dipped a filbert brush into the turps and wiped it off with a rag, while staring at one of the large canvases on the easels, assemblages of bodies, wedged into each other to form gothic peaks.

Pashone swiped a dab of paint with his brush from his palette and began to flick highlights onto the foreheads and shoulders of his painted figures. He was suddenly seized with pain. He gripped his left arm without dropping his brush, nor rag.

Pashone grimaced as he struggled against the heart attack, struggling to complete the placement of the constellation of highlights on the painting, on an elbow, the side of a nose, until he ultimately fell, dropping to the floor.

*

Deep in the Malibu hills, the air was sweet with surf air. Trees and their leaves caught the final embers of a setting sun.

A squad of men in jumpsuits slammed up the doors on two unmarked vans. One handyman banged on the side of his van, and they all drove out through the gates onto the private road that serpentined out to PCH, where the waves lulled the shore.

Inside the house, a couple of floors beneath the surface, wealthy eccentric Bobby Werner stood in silhouette in front of a newly framed Matisse, enormous cocktail in hand.

He swirled his drink and pondered the drawing for a moment before collapsing into a silent cackle and slapping himself on the thigh. He sank into a plush recliner and just stared. He would stare for hours. *He gets what he wants*, he thought to himself.

Bobby thought of calling Tobin. Maybe Tobin knew of some interesting people who might enjoy viewing a rare and secret Matisse.

*

Kevin studied his advanced physics, his piles of books, occupying only half of the large, round Carrows booth. Two of his textbooks were wrapped in US Army book covers. He tore small pieces off the corner of a sheet of paper and ate them.

He was solemn. He had seen his best friend Digger drift away.

It started when Digger stopped taking classes at the junior college. Digger had always had a chasm —don't we all?— but his just seemed lately to deepen, to widen.

That was Digger's choice, he told himself.

Kevin's Coke needed a refill. He looked all around, but there was no sign of Karen. Another waitress, Doris, arrived at Kevin's table, informing him that she would be taking over this station.

Karen had gone home for the night.

The next day, Kevin's mother drove him to the recruiting station, where a bus waited for the line of new recruits. His twin sisters sat this one out. They were out getting piercings or pregnant. Kevin and Mom got out of the car, then they exchanged hugs, and he climbed aboard. Through the window, they exchanged waves, and Mom blew kisses. The bus let out a loud Pssst! as if it were about to let out a juicy secret.

*

The kitchen in Digger's old house was now spotless. The place was silent.

His sister, Audrey, had been cleaning for hours, and now she was pooped.

"If it wasn't for me, the place would be a fuckin' sty," she said aloud.

Wearing a sweaty bandana, Audrey pulled off her yellow rubber gloves and went to her bedroom. A shower sounded just great right now.

Digger was gone. What was a tug of war when the other side just drops their end of the rope? Sure, she was glad, but... things just felt different.

Wait a minute.

She found an unmarked envelope left on her bed. She opened it to find it stuffed with several large bills. There was enough for a down payment and a first and last on an apartment. Her look of surprise was hardly perceptible... but it was there.

*

Bridget came home from cosmetology school with a mortarboard on her head and balloons in her fist. It was graduation day, and the school was closed for a party. Bridget had allowed herself two pieces of cake. (It was a good cake.)

Her mom was home and gave her a big hug, told her she had mail. Bridget looked through the pile. Bill. Bill. Junk. Bill. Wait.

There was a large envelope with no postage, no address. It just read, "Bridget."

When she opened it, the contents made tears squirt out of her eyes. She made a muffled squeal. *Oh, shut up!* she said to herself.

It was two first-class airline tickets to Barcelona and twenty $100 bills.

She knew many, many people who would do this, but not many who *could.* It was not only the sweetest gesture, but the kindest *act.* She was baffled. She was grateful. She was humbled.

*

As he approached the First Class check-in counter, Digger, smartly but comfortably dressed, opened his new, long, leather Continental wallet for his boarding pass. It was beneath a deposit draft for a numbered offshore account and some very large foreign bills.

"Andalusia, Spain, one-way. Must be nice." The young auburn-haired ticket woman had an interesting face and a clear touch of self-consciousness.

"I've never been. You have lovely cheekbones," observed Digger.

He skimmed a letter accepting him into the Design Center full-time and tossed it into the trash bin next to the kiosk.

Taken aback, the ticket woman shook her head no.

"Here. Let me show you."

Digger took out a small Moleskine sketchbook and a Mont Blanc pen from his suit pocket.

On the countertop, Digger scratched out a delicate sketch of Ticket Woman. It was flattering, but not dishonest, not in the least.

He carefully, gently, and expertly tore it out and handed it to her.

She looked upon it. They exchanged kind looks.

"Would you sign it for me?"

"Of course."

With only a stylish shoulder bag, a suit bag, a small book of Spanish phrases, a small, brown bottle, and a brand-new passport, Digger disappeared onto a plane. The pressurized air ducts accepted him with the breath of a mechanical dragon.

About the Author

Stephen "Burpo" Debonrepos was born and raised in Southern California, where he worked as a storyboard illustrator for the Television, Motion Picture, and Advertising industries. He is a graduate of Art Center College of Design and Mount San Antonio College. He is the author of the graphic novel CRUSH for Aeon Press as well as the volume of self-published poetry New Old Stuff, available on Amazon.

He lives in Southern CA with his lifetime girlfriend and their cats.

If you enjoyed this book, we would appreciate it if you could take a moment to leave a review on Amazon.

If you enjoyed this book, we would appreciate it if you could take a moment to leave a review on Amazon.

Other Books by the Author:

NEW OLD STUFF – Poems

https://bit.ly/3K24s1n